"Okay, we've been waiting for you, honey," Coach Turner said, smiling broadly, almost leering at Cass. She just wanted to get out of there as fast as she could, but everyone was watching her, waiting to see her fall on her face, and she wasn't going to give them the satisfaction.

"What position did you say you played, doll?" Coach Turner asked condescendingly.

"I didn't say," Cass answered.

The boys began snickering.

"Well, are you going to tell us, or doesn't the girls' team have assigned positions?" the coach asked sarcastically.

"I played forward," Cass answered, "but I've been playing guard for the past few months—just in case."

"Then let's see what kind of speed you have," the coach roared, and Cass stepped into place....

Fawcett Juniper Books
by Marilyn Levy:

THE GIRL IN THE PLASTIC CAGE

LIFE IS NOT A DRESS REHEARSAL

LOVE IS A LONG SHOT

Marilyn Levy

FAWCETT JUNIPER • NEW YORK

RLI: VL: Grades 5 + up
      IL: Grades 6 + up

A Fawcett Juniper Book
Published by Ballantine Books
Copyright © 1986 by Marilyn Levy

Library of Congress Catalog Card Number: 86-90899

ISBN 0-449-70150-6

Printed in Canada

First Edition: September 1986

Many thanks to Elliot Turret and
Rafael Caceres for their help.

CHAPTER ONE

"Toss it here," Cass yelled, racing into the gym. Coach Morris whirled around, momentarily startled, then chuckled and threw the ball at Cass, who grabbed it and leaped high into the air, eyes on the basket, carefully shooting the ball and laughing as it rippled through the net in one clean motion and bounced to the floor.

"Good shot, Carothers," the coach said, walking to the middle of the court and slapping Cass on the back. "You must have been practicing over the summer."

"Only about three hours a day," Cass mumbled, grinning.

"Looks like you grew a few inches, too," Coach Morris added, standing back, carefully measuring Cass. "I think you must be three inches taller than I am."

"Three and a half," Cass said. "I think I'll break six feet by basketball season."

"You're gonna break more than six feet," Coach Morris bragged confidently. "You're going to break every league record, then you're gonna show 'em what Santa Monica High School can do at the championship game."

"Yeah, I hope so," Cass said softly, picking up the ball and shooting another basket.

"You're the best player I've ever worked with, Carothers. The most confident, the most determined, and the most disciplined. You know what you want, and you go for it. I like that."

"Thanks," Cass said, barely able to look the coach in the eye.

"I've been grooming this team for three years, and this year it's all going to pay off. You guys are going to bring home that trophy for me. I know it! I know it! I know it! I can smell that sweet smell of victory," Coach Morris yelled, grabbing the ball from Cass and tossing it into the air.

Cass watched the ball rim the basket for a moment, then drop through almost haltingly.

"Coach," Cass began, trying to recall that famous confidence which had suddenly ducked out the back door, leaving a gurgle of confusion in its place.

"Yeah, Carothers?"

"Listen—I—ah—I think the team's gonna be great this year. You're right. We will win the championship game 'cause we have so many top players," Cass said with a phony enthusiasm. "McCleary, Rogers, Weinberg, Lowery, and Gaynes have all been on the team for three years. You've never had so many seniors ready to play before."

"*We*, Carothers. *We've* never had so many seniors. We're a team. We work together. This isn't a game for prima donnas. This is a team sport."

"Yeah," Cass said, feeling like a latter-day Atlas, suddenly understanding exactly how he must have felt with the weight of the world on his shoulders.

"But I gotta add," Coach Morris admitted with a smile and a friendly punch to Cass's right arm, "if we did have stars on our team, and if I had to pick a player I couldn't do without, it would be you, Carothers."

"Come on, Coach—"

"No—I mean it. I mean it, and I can say that to you because I know what kind of kid you are. I know it's not something you'd go blabbing around, because I know the team means more to you than individual stardom. Right, Carothers?"

"Right, Coach. Right," Cass said, bouncing the ball slowly across the court, walking toward the door, hoping to get out before the coach could say anything else.

"Carothers," Coach Morris yelled, "if your head was any closer to the ground, you'd be sweepin' up the floor with your hair. Come back here and tell me what the hell is eatin' you."

"Nothing," Cass said and walked out.

Coach Morris followed Cass into the parking lot and opened the door of the '72 Dodge Dart, which was Cass's prize possession. Cass sat slumped in the driver's seat, leaning against the steering wheel.

"Okay. Come on, Carothers. Let's have it. What's going on?"

Cass got out of the car, leaving the door open. She walked over to the hood, plopped down on it, and, staring into space for a few minutes, tried to figure out how to break the news to the coach. This wasn't going to be easy, and it didn't feel very good, either. The coach was terrific—kind, generous, understanding, a great athlete, someone you could always count on. How could Cass cop out now? How could anyone let the coach down?

"You didn't fail Algebra did you?" the coach asked, suddenly panic-stricken. "You haven't been disqualified, have you?"

"I got a B in Algebra, thanks to your tutoring," Cass answered.

"Got problems at home, Cass?" Coach Morris asked gently.

"No, just the usual," Cass sighed.

"Well, then, are you gonna tell me what it is, or are we going to play Twenty Questions?"

"I can't play on the team this year," Cass blurted out.

"Whooo. Slow down a little. You passed Algebra. Pass everything else?" the coach asked, cautiously.

"Yes."

"No trouble at home."

"Right."

"You're in great form, so that isn't it."

"Right," Cass agreed again, unable simply to say what had to be said, wishing the conversation would just play itself out and end.

"Carothers, you're driving me crazy," Coach Morris yelled, flopping down on the hood of the car next to Cass. "How bad can it be? Let's have it. Maybe we can do something about it."

"This is very difficult," Cass said slowly. "I mean, no one's been better to me than you have. I owe you a whole lot, and—and I hate to let you down, is all."

Cass stared into space, trying to get up enough nerve to come out with it and wondering how to appease the coach so that the transition would be as easy as possible.

Preparing a speech, then quickly rejecting it, Cass coughed and beat the hood of the car with a steady rhythm. "When in doubt, go for the truth," the coach always said.

"I want to play on the boys' team this season," Cass finally admitted, unable to think of any other way to say it.

"You what?" Coach Morris shouted, leaping off the hood of the car.

"Look, I know how this must sound. You probably think I don't care about our team, but I do. Really, I do, and if Weinstein wasn't as good a forward as I am—better even, probably, I mean, she will be anyway—I wouldn't even think about switching, but,

Coach—I'm gonna graduate in June, and the only way I'm going to college—a good school, anyway—is on a basketball scholarship."

"Yeah, I know that, Carothers," Coach Morris said, shaking her head. "I know that. Scouts have been watching you for over a year. The gym will be crawling with them for our big game."

"Yeah, but they've been watching a lot of other players, too. The competition is fierce these days. I need to do something to show those damn scouts that I'm a little better, a little different, a little gutsier than the competition. Those scouts may be watching me, but, even at six feet, I'm not going to stand out next to a player like Cheryl Miller."

"But the team—"

"I know. I'm sorry. Believe me. I spent a lot of time thinking about this, and it was a painful decision. McCleary and I talked about it for five hours one night. She's the one who finally helped me make up my mind. I've gone as far as I can go on the girls' team. I need to sharpen my skills against players who are better than I am."

Coach Morris slumped down on the hood of the car.

"Besides, all the other girls' parents can help them out after they graduate," Cass said. "You know—"

"I know, Cass," the coach said, with less edge in her voice.

"Hell, Saint and Sky borrow money from *me*. I mean, I love my parents, but I'll probably wind up supporting them, and I have to find some way—the best way I can—to get an education so I can do that."

Cass could feel tears beginning to well up in her eyes, and everything began to look slightly blurred, but she bit her lip hard and silently chastised herself for being such a big baby. She forced the tears to recede. She hated letting the coach down. She hated

letting the team down, the girls she had played basketball with since eighth grade. But what could she
do? She had to protect herself. She had to think about
her future. She knew from experience what happens
to people who live only in the present, without making
plans for tomorrow, or the next day, or the next year.
She was not going to be one of those people who
couldn't profit from history, not even from their own
personal history. The coach was right. She was disciplined, and she did know what she wanted. She also
had the guts to go after it. She had to. Either that or
stay buried in the past, like her parents, which was
okay for them because it was their past. But it wasn't
hers. She wasn't a flower child, and she never would
be. Although her parents had been shocked to discover
her competitiveness, Cass had decided very early that
she liked to win, and if that made her parents unhappy,
she was sorry. She would try to understand their choices,
but they would also have to understand hers. Luckily,
one of the things they believed in was freedom, in the
extreme sense. Some people even called it anarchy,
but her parents agreed that each person had to work
out his or her own karma, not fight it, and if Cass had
to be competitive to work out her karma, well, they
were even willing to go along with that.

"I can't tell you I'm happy about your choice," the
coach said, turning away from Cass.

"I can understand that," Cass said.

"I've been grooming this team for a long time. It
won't be the same without you," the coach said, turning back to look at Cass.

"It won't be the same without you, either," Cass
said, hoping the coach believed her, hoping that somehow she would understand that it wasn't that she was
rejecting the coach or the team, it was that she was
representing all of them. She would show everybody

what a good coach could do with a scrawny, shy girl who had walked awkwardly into the high school gym three years ago, hoping to be noticed. "I'll be playing out there for all of us," Cass said, her blue eyes meeting the coach's for the first time.

"Pretty confident, aren't you, Carothers?" the coach asked, erasing the frown from her face, smiling at Cass.

"Got that from you, Coach," Cass said, relieved, teasing the coach and meaning it at the same time.

"So, what do you want me to do?" Coach Morris asked.

"Get me on the boys' team, of course."

"Oh, no, that's adding insult to injury. First she tells me she's not going to be on my team—"

"I thought it was our team—"

"Okay, first she tells me she's not going to be on *our* team, then she asks me to help her defect. You crazy or something, Carothers?"

"Kind of," Cass said, happy, now, knowing that the coach would give in sooner or later, knowing the coach was just teasing, stringing her along, and also knowing that the coach knew it, too. They had been more than coach and student; they had been friends, and the coach had always been there when Cass needed a friend. She knew Coach Morris wouldn't walk away from her, now.

"And I bet you even want me to talk to Turner for you, don't you?"

"Yeah."

"Oh, no! Oh, no. No. No. No. That's asking for a supreme sacrifice. If you want to play on that—that—male—that boys' team, you talk to him."

"But he won't listen to me."

"That's right. He won't listen to me, either."

"But you're a teacher."

"A female teacher."

"You gotta," Cass begged.

"No, I don't gotta," Coach Morris said, laughing. Then she paused for a moment and scratched her head, pulling loose her dark hair which was piled high on top of it. She frowned deeply, sighed, then slowly smiled at Cass, who looked at her expectantly. "I don't gotta, but I will," the coach said.

"You won't be sorry," Cass yelled, as she ran around to Coach Morris's side of the car and gave her a hug.

"Oh, yes, I will," the coach said, "but that's my problem. Check with me after school starts. Turner's not back from vacation yet."

"Thanks," Cass said softly. "I wouldn't be where I am without you, ya know."

"I know," the coach answered, as she absentmindedly put her whistle in her mouth and started jogging back toward the gym with a determined stride.

Cass watched her run until she turned into the gym door. Her heart beat fast. She was happy. Hell, she was ecstatic. No girl at Samohi had ever played on the boys' basketball team. She had crossed the first hurdle, and she was on her way to making history; but, she felt sort of lonely, standing there in the barren parking lot. Suddenly, the tears which she had been able to control just a few minutes ago, came splashing out of her eyes. There was an empty feeling in her stomach, even though she had won her first battle. She knew why the coach hadn't turned around to wave good-bye.

"I'll miss you, too," Cass whispered to herself, her eyes still on the gym door, hoping to catch one last glimpse of the coach.

Leaning against her car, she stood there for a long time. When she finally looked away, she noticed Julio Martinez walking toward her, carrying a gym bag. He smiled hesitantly, shyly, in spite of the fact that they had sat next to each other in English class all last year. Julio had probably come to shoot a few baskets, get in some practice before school started. He had been voted the most valuable player on the boys' team last year, and he took the game as seriously as Cass did.

"Got a cold?" he asked, as he squinted, shielding his dark brown eyes from the late afternoon sun.

"Sort of," Cass said, suddenly tongue-tied. God, she wished she could think of a more clever response.

"Well, take care," Julio said, walking away.

Cass wanted to call him back, wanted to say something else, get him to stay and talk to her, to fill up the parking lot with his presence so it wouldn't be so empty. She liked Julio. She liked his dark, brooding good looks, his finely chiseled Mexican features with their ancestral Indian heritage; his sturdy, solid body, a sharp contrast to her own slender wispy blondness. She was curious about him. He was always alone, except when he played basketball. He didn't seem to hang out with the other Mexican students, and he didn't hang around with anyone else, either. Well, maybe she'd get to know him better when she got to play on the team. Correction, she cautioned herself, smiling. *If* she got to play on the team. She couldn't afford to be too cocky about it, yet. There was still a major hurdle to get over before she suited up with the Wildcats.

CHAPTER TWO

Cass revved up the motor of the old Dart, named
Willie Boy, after William Faulkner. She figured if her
parents could name her McCaslin, after a character in
the Faulkner story they were reading the night she was
conceived, she could go one better and name her "baby"
after the original. Actually, she had to admit there was
some hostility in christening the car Willie Boy, but
who wouldn't feel hostile after having to listen, year
after year, to snickers on each first day of classes when
the teachers call the roll? Every September, Cass
patiently would ask her teachers to call her Cass, not
McCaslin, and eventually they would remember, and
the snickers would die down. Still, Cass had always
wished her parents had been reading *Jane Eyre* the
night she was conceived, instead of a Faulkner novel.

"Come on, Willie Boy," she whispered, as she
maneuvered the tan tanker out of the parking lot. "Even
if you are an old man, you're still cherry," she said,
smiling, as she sped along Ocean Avenue toward the
Pacific Coast Highway. Willie Boy had been Cass's
gift to herself, last year. She had waited tables at the
Inn of the Seventh Ray, up the road from where she
lived in Topanga Canyon, and had saved all her tips
in order to buy the car. Her parents hadn't been any
too happy about it, either. Neither of them drove. They
didn't believe in polluting the air any more than it was
already polluted, so they kept two horses in a barn

near the house, which was one of the reasons they lived in the canyon. It was the last bastion of hippie-dom in the Los Angeles area. After flower power had finally wilted in Venice, and it had become too expensive and too difficult to live in the more desirable areas, Saint Simon, Cass's father, and Sky, her mother, had built their own cabin in the woods in Topanga Canyon. Cass liked it there. It was free and clean and very beautiful, even if it was a bit isolated. With a car, however, she could make it to school in twenty minutes. So she had the best of all possible worlds. The only problem was that in winter when the rains were sometimes merciless, the coastal highway was closed, and she had to drive over the mountains to the valley, and then cross over the valley, back to the west side, to get to school. All of this took a couple of hours, assuming she could get her car out of the muddy driveway and down the canyon road in the first place.

Cass glanced at her watch as she shifted lanes to make the right turn up Topanga Canyon Road. She still had time to relax before she had to go to work. She was glad she had worked five shifts a week all summer. This would free her to concentrate on basketball once school started. She could cut back to one shift a week—Sunday brunch. That wouldn't interfere with any games or practices. And actually, she didn't really mind working at the Inn. Everybody was very nice—a little too nice, in fact. It got on her nerves sometimes, but it was a pleasant, if bland, place to be, and the chimes tinkling in the breeze and the candles, with their faintly religious aura, made her feel good, even though she didn't accept the pseudo born-again ideas of the couple who owned the place. Having lived with Sky and Saint Simon all these years had taught her not to rush into accepting anyone's religious beliefs—born again or not. In the past few years, if she could remember correctly, her parents had embraced Buddhism with a passion, rejected it, and had then gone on to become Sikhs for a while. Sky, however, had found the high headdresses too cumbersome, and the conversion hadn't taken hold. Cass was secretly glad, since she hated to admit she was embarrassed by anything her parents strongly believed in—for the moment—but she couldn't help thinking that, with their cylindrical turbans, they had looked an awful lot like the Coneheads, whom she watched on *Saturday Night Live* reruns at her friend Kathy McCleary's house. The Carothers, of course, had no TV of their own.

Thinking about her parents, Cass smiled as she pulled into the driveway leading to the house. It was really more of a dirt road than a driveway, but it served its purpose. Chickens scattered in every direction as the car wound up the hill toward the cabin, which had become more elaborate in the past few years as Saint Simon added a room here and there, and had filled it with smooth-textured furniture that he had either built or refinished. Sky came running after the chickens, addressing each one of them separately, with the same sense of dignity Adam must have felt when he named the first animals. Whatever Sky did, she did with dignity, and she never ever felt silly or foolish, as most people would. Cass had to admire her for that. Actually, she had to admire her mother for lots of things, Cass thought, as she watched the chickens run to Sky, clucking away as if they understood her and were responding. They seemed to know that they wouldn't end up cooking in a soup or roasting in an oven. They were there to produce eggs, and produce they did. Day after day, Sky swept through the area, picking up fresh eggs, which she sold to the market at the foot of the canyon.

"Hi, honey," Sky said, wafting up to the car. Sky

never quite walked. In her long skirts, which grazed the ground as she glided by, she always looked as if she were floating. She had the same long blond hair that Cass had, and the same gentle, ethereal looks. Her hands, like Cass's, were large and powerful, however, and seemed incongruous with the rest of her body, which was small and slight. But while Cass's hands were powerful because of athletics, her mother's hands had hoed and cultivated the land which, like the chickens, seemed to thrive under her touch. Name it, Sky grew it in her pesticide-free garden. She had tomatoes, green beans, zucchini, artichokes, corn, and herbs of all kinds—anise, basil, chives, and mint. She pruned the fruit trees herself and picked and squeezed fresh oranges and grapefruit into juice. At times, she seemed to tickle the fruit and vegetables into producing for her, cooing over them, singing to them, offering them thanks. Whatever it was she did, Cass thought that Sky ought to share her wisdom with the farmers of America.

Cass slid out of her car and kissed her mother.

"Well?" Sky asked.

"Guess." Cass answered.

"Tell me," Sky said, grabbing Cass's hands.

"Just intuit it, like you do everything else," Cass said, laughing.

"She's going to talk to the boys' coach for you."

"*Yeahhhhhhh*," Cass said, beaming.

"I'm so proud of you, honey. Saint and I are going to come to that championship football game, even if we're in the middle of a serious fast."

"Basketball, Mom," Cass said, laughing.

"Oh, well, it's the thought that counts. Right?"

"Right," Cass said, putting her arm around her mother. "What's to eat? I'm starving."

"Well, actually—" Sky said, blanching a little, "I

was so busy reading all that material I got from Michael—"

"Michael?" Cass asked, frowning. This was a new one.

"The Hasid I'm studying with now."

"Hasid?"

"Jewish mysticism."

"Sky! You promised."

"I know. I know. I'm really sorry."

"You forgot to pay the bills again, didn't you, Sky?"

"Well—"

"So they turned off the electricity and the gas, right?"

"But they'll turn them on again as soon as we give them the money," Sky said.

"You mean, as soon as I take the money down to them, don't you?"

"Well, it would be faster if you drove, wouldn't it?"

"I'll have to do it tomorrow," Cass said glumly.

"But I did make a wonderful fruit salad," Sky said, brightening up, "and a wonderful vegetable salad," she added. "You'll love them. Really," she said eagerly, her eyes shining, her smile flooding her lovely face with sunshine. No wonder the chickens gave eggs, and the vegetables grew, and the fruits blossomed, Cass thought. Who could be angry with Sky for more than a minute, and who could ever say no to her?

"That sounds great, Mom," Cass said, giving Sky a hug. "Don't worry about the bills. I'll take care of them."

"I love you, Cass," Sky said, returning her daughter's hug. "You're a terrific kid—only—I wish you were my mother."

"I am," Cass answered, laughing. "Or at least I must have been in another life," Cass said half jokingly.

"Of course you were, darling," her mother answered seriously.

"Of course," Cass said, biting her bottom lip till it hurt.

"Let's go get Saint and tell him to take a break," Sky said, pulling Cass along with her as they walked toward a smaller version of the cabin, built about a hundred feet from the house. This cabin was one room, which most people would have used for a garage, but Saint used it for a workshop and hideaway. It was cozy, warm, and sunny, with lots of windows, a fire place, and a cot with an Indian spread and lots of pillows on it. Cass liked to go out there in the winter, to build a fire and read with the smell of the newly sanded wood in her nostrils. Luckily, her father stripped and varnished outside, so the cabin remained a haven, filled with all kinds of tools and equipment.

When Cass and her mother ducked under a climbing rosebush into an area which had been cleared away for the cabin, they spotted Saint. Saint's given name was Simon, but his friends had begun calling him Saint Simon during the sixties. Eventually, they had dropped the Simon, and now he was simply called Saint, or the Saint, by everyone who knew him. He stood in the sun, stripped to the waist, wearing an old pair of jeans, faded, torn, and baggy on the bottom—a remnant from his earlier life, no doubt. His wavy brown hair was pulled loosely back into a pony tail, which rested on the back of his neck and hung between his shoulder blades. Standing there, totally engrossed in sanding the old, carved, wooden chair, he did, indeed, look like a saint. The late afternoon sun formed a halo around his head as he whistled a hymn to his idol, repeating the refrain from "Yesterday," an old Paul McCartney song, over and over again until it became a litany, his litany, a dedication to his particular reality.

No, Saint would never listen to a new McCartney album. Bringing a Paul McCartney solo album into the house would definitely be considered heresy.

"'Oh, I believe in yesterday,'" the Saint ended with a flourish. He always sang the last line, even if he had whistled the rest of it. Having completed his daily ritual, he smiled.

Sky and Cass ran over to him and put their arms around him. They're both a little nuts, Cass thought, but she wouldn't trade her parents for anything. Of course, she did wish they were just a tiny bit more materialistic. It was one thing to do work which made you happy and was fullfilling, but she didn't quite understand why that prevented her parents from thinking about the future, at least occasionally. She sighed. I guess if you want your kids to be straight, you should be as far out as possible. Cass would never think of taking drugs, though they were openly stashed all over the house. She knew they would ruin her body and eventually fry her brain, but Sky and Saint just smoked away, oblivious to any possible harm. Hell, Sky even grew sinsemilla in her garden, and it flourished just as abundantly as all her other plants. They never did cocaine, though, which seemed to be the new "hip" drug for the upwardly mobile executive-type parents of the kids she knew at school. Sky and Saint would never be caught dead doing anything that was 1980's hip.

"Have a good day, sunshine?" Saint asked Cass, as he gave her a hug. Her father had a dozen nicknames for her—sunshine, rose bud, flower child, moonbeam. He hardly ever called her by her real name. Maybe the marijuana had gotten to his head, after all, and he just couldn't remember it, Cass thought suddenly.

"Who am I?" she demanded to know.

Sky and Saint exchanged a long, sad look.

"Don't worry, sweet pea," Saint said. "Everybody goes through this kind of identity crisis every now and then. I'm surprised it's taken you this long."

Cass started to laugh. She wasn't ever going to change them, and she really didn't even want to try.

CHAPTER THREE

"Suit up. Turner's finally agreed to let you work out with the boys," Coach Morris said when Cass walked into her office after school, as she had every day for the past two months.

"Great. Oh-mi-god. That's great," Cass shouted, throwing her books into the air. "Now? Wait a minute. You mean, now?"

"Now."

"But I'm not ready now. I mean, I thought it would take a few more days, you know. I need some time to think about it, to get ready."

"You've been thinking about nothing else, Cass."

"Yeah, but—"

"You get one chance, Carothers, and this is it. Now get in there and show that turkey all the stuff I've been teaching you for the past three years."

"But, what if—"

"No what-if's or why-not's or maybe's," the coach said, shoving Cass out of her office. "The basketball court in fifteen minutes."

"Okay, okay," Cass said, reluctantly leaving the familiar warmth of the coach's office. She glanced back one more time, but the coach was busy shuffling papers around on her desk. "Well, aren't you even going to wish me luck or anything?" she asked, disappointed and dismayed at the coach's cavalier attitude.

"Of course I'm not going to wish you luck. You don't need luck out there. You need skill. With luck you make one basket, maybe two, during a game. It takes skill to really play basketball, and you know it."

"Well, geez. How about a little moral support then?" Cass pleaded.

"You got it. Now get out of here before you blow the whole thing."

Cass walked slowly to the locker room. Okay, so this was her big chance. Then why was she feeling so depressed? All right, she could understand Coach Morris's not wanting to make a big deal out of this. She was probably upset about her not playing on the girls' team, after all. She probably secretly hoped that Cass would blow the tryout and wind up back with her. Nah, the coach wouldn't be so mean-spirited. Or would she? The coach had set it up for her, hadn't she? Maybe I should just go back and tell her I want to forget about the whole damn thing, Cass thought. It was a stupid idea, anyway.

Cass turned around and started walking back to Coach Morris's office. She got halfway there and stopped. "You're the one who half hopes you'll blow it and wind up back on the girls' team," she said to herself. "You're just scared, Cass Carothers. Pull yourself together." She sighed. "Easier said than done," she whispered, as she turned to walk back to the locker room.

She sat there giving herself a pep talk as she laced up her high tops. "Listen, jerk, you only get once chance. People would die for a chance like this. How many girls have the ability and guts to get even this far?" She felt better. "So you don't make it," she continued. "So what? At least, you gave it your best shot."

Cass jumped up from the bench. She smiled and

walked toward the gym, dribbling a basketball for moral support. "I'm ready," she said. "Hell, I'm as ready as I'm ever going to be, and I'm going to show those guys what McCaslin Carothers can do."

As Cass was about to dance onto the basketball court, exuding all the self-confidence for which she was known around school, she saw Coach Turner talking to the boys. Probably warning them not to give me a real workout, she thought, amused. He doesn't know the kind of training we're used to.

"So, this broad is going to practice with us today, see," she heard him say.

Cass stopped walking and stood at the door to the gym, frozen. All eyes were on the coach. Nobody saw her. She could just walk out, or make some noise so they'd all know she was there. No, she couldn't. She couldn't move. She couldn't speak. She just stood there as the team hooted and howled at Turner's announcement.

"Okay, okay, you suckers," Turner said, waving his hands in the air. The team kept laughing and yelling at him. Finally, he blew his whistle and they all settled down—somewhat. "Okay, that's better. Now listen. Okay, you're right to laugh your heads off about this, but there's nothing I could do. See? You want to play basketball, you gotta make compromises once in a while, play politics," he shouted, angrily. "Even if it is against my better judgment," he added, almost to himself.

Cass was stunned as she listened to the groans and complaints of the team. Somehow, this was one thing she hadn't counted on, or even given a second thought.

"Hey, give the broad a chance, suckers—but don't let her get away with shit—and clean up your language when she comes out here," he yelled. Then, he turned around and spotted Cass.

"Okay, so we've been waiting for you, honey," he said, smiling broadly, almost leering at her. It made her stomach turn. She felt truly ill. She just wanted to get out of there as fast as she could, but everyone was watching her, waiting to see her fall on her face, and she wasn't going to give them the satisfaction.

"What position did you say you played, doll?" Coach Turner asked condescendingly.

"I didn't say," Cass answered, finding her voice from some place way down inside and bringing it up with great effort.

The boys began snickering.

"Well, are you going to tell us, or doesn't the girls' team have assigned positions?" the coach asked sarcastically.

"I played forward," Cass answered, "but I've been playing guard for the past few months, in case—just in case," she said, barely moving her mouth.

"Then let's see what kind of speed you have," he roared. "Everybody to the baseline for suicides."

The team got into position on either side of the hoop as the coach called line drills. Cass stepped into place next to Julio, last in line on the right side of the basket. Weiner ran quickly to the first line and back and was followed by Anderson and Jackson. Knowing she was as fast as anyone else, Cass finally took her turn. Coach Turner blew his whistle and called next for a timed line drill. "If any guy can't make it under thirty seconds, all of you will have to run the lines again," he added. Once more, everyone got into position and ran as fast as he/she could to the first line, back to the basket, to the second line, and back again. Most of the boys were panting for breath, since this was a difficult work out. After they all finished, they waited for Coach Turner to comment.

"Okay, let's do it again," he yelled. The team

groaned. They hated line drills. "How come?" Weiner protested. "Because Carothers made it in thirty-five seconds," the coach said, smiling faintly. Like hell, Cass thought. She had been as swift as anyone out there. But she knew she couldn't prove it. She had worked out all summer. She had timed herself again and again. She knew she had made it in under thirty seconds, but she got back in position with the rest of the team and prepared to run it again.

"Okay, let's run the stairs," Turner shouted, when they had finished.

"Shit," Jackson said under his breath. "I hate stairs." Weiner and Anderson began walking to the bleachers, and everybody followed. After a few minutes, the team began looking at the coach, expecting him to blow the whistle indicating they were through with this warm-up; but he just stood there, frowning, watching them go through the motions. Cass knew what he was doing. He was trying to tire her out, and he was doing a good job of it, too, but he was doing an even better job on the other guys. Finally, the whistle blew. Sweat glistened on everyone's forehead as they all ground slowly to a halt, walked to the gym floor, and collapsed.

"Hey, you pansies," the coach shouted, "let's get up there for some free throws. Whad' ya think this is? A tea party, or something?"

Cass glanced around at the wall of faces in front of her. She knew all of them; many of the kids on the team were in her classes. But suddenly they looked hostile and threatening, waiting to pounce on her, holding back their laughter. She caught Julio's eye for a moment. He appeared to be uncomfortable and looked away. Weiner, Jackson, Anderson, and the other boys lined up for the free throws. Jackson was standing in front of the net with the ball when the coach yelled for Cass to go first. Before she got into position, Jackson shot her the ball. She reached out for it and missed. "Try again," Weiner snapped, grabbing it up and tossing it to her. This time she caught it and dribbled it to the basket. She was shaking. She tried to calm herself. Steady. Steady, she thought. You've done this before. You've done this a million times. You know how to handle pressure. Just look at the basket and shoot. Shoot! She shot. The ball rimmed the basket and bounced off the side. She saw Jackson and Weiner nudge each other and make faces.

"Try it again," Julio said quietly, as he tossed her the ball.

She caught the smirk on the coach's face as she lifted the ball in the air. This time, she missed the basket by a mile.

"Let's get on with it," the coach said wearily, as Jackson stepped up to the net.

The rest of the team made their throws easily, and once again the coach blew his whistle. More drills followed. Then they broke down the offensive plays and worked on them. Finally, Coach Turner yelled, "Shirts and skins. Carothers you get in there with— ah—Weiner." Weiner, of course, Cass thought. "Jackson," Coach Turner continued. Sure, she sighed to herself. "Martinez." Well, that wasn't too bad. At least he doesn't seem as hostile, Cass decided. The coach rattled off the players, dividing them into two teams.

"Weiner's team, skins. Steven's team, shirts." Everybody started to roar as Weiner, Jackson, Anderson, and Raden took off their shirts. Cass stood there, burning with anger.

"Oh, so sorry," Coach Turner said, bowing, "I forgot. Weiner's team, shirts. Steven's team, skins. Now let's play."

Cass's team huddled around Weiner, who began giving them instructions. The boys carefully avoided touching Cass in any way, though they slapped and patted each other. Cass was too nervous to listen. She hoped she could get by on her instincts even though she knew instinctive basketball playing was not Coach Morris's idea of how to play the game. However, at this point, she had no choice other than limping back to the locker room, which didn't seem like such a bad idea to her.

"Foul, Carothers," the coach called as Cass bumped into Stevens. "But—" she started to say, then dropped it. She knew that Stevens had made it look as if she had bumped into him. He had actually bumped into her. Now she knew how Mary Decker must have felt at the Olympics.

This is too much, she thought. It just isn't worth it. She was ready to throw in the towel when she heard a familiar voice call out: "Go, Carothers. Show those macho mothers what you've got." Cass, who was guarding Julio Martinez, suddenly grabbed the ball, leaving him stunned, and ran with it. She jumped up and poured it into the basket. Julio remained standing in place on the floor, dumbfounded. She had swept it up so fast that he still didn't understand what had happened.

"Wow, Julio," Weiner hooted.

"That-a-way, babe," Jackson called, swinging his ass provocatively.

"What are you gonna do when we play with a real team, Martinez?" Stevens shouted, laughing.

The whole team was roaring. Cass wanted to hold her ears tightly to block out the sound. The coach was blowing away madly on his whistle, but no one was paying attention. They were jumping up and down, practically standing on their stupid heads, pointing to Julio, who was rooted to the spot, humiliated beyond belief. Cass sneaked a look at him out of the corner of her eye. She cringed. She was so sorry, but she was not sorry enough to want to take back what she had done. She was damn proud of what she had just done. She knew that she was out there on that floor by herself. She knew she had one chance to prove herself, and she was going to do it. She grabbed the ball from Raden, who was dribbling it lazily, and she ran back to the basket. She threw the ball in, and it came slamming down, right back into her hands. She threw it up again and again, making basket after basket, fending off the rest of the team, moving so fast they couldn't grab the ball away from her. They were so afraid of touching her, they wouldn't get near her, and she used that for all it was worth.

Coach Morris was cheering wildly. Cass glanced over at her, just in time to catch Coach Turner throw her a dirty look.

"Go get 'em, Carothers," Coach Morris yelled in response to Turner. "I knew you could do it."

Cass beamed and threw the ball to Weiner. She could now afford to give it up to someone else. She wanted to show them she could also be a team member, not just a star.

Weiner caught the ball and took it to the hoop for a lay-up. The ball was inbounded to Martinez, who dribbled it a few times, then slammed it against the wall and walked off the court.

CHAPTER FOUR

Sweating from every pore, Cass jogged back to the showers. The rest of the team quietly headed for the boys' locker room. She could faintly hear them talking and swearing, since only a wall separated the two rooms. They were a hell of a lot less enthusiastic than when they had jeeringly waited for her to make a fool of herself. She turned on the water full blast to wash away their voices. Their attitude, their obvious lack of acceptance, was spoiling her triumph. She wanted to remember the way she had made basket after basket. She didn't want to remember the team's snide remarks and sneering glances as they walked off the court.

She soaped herself all over, trying to wash away the hurt she felt at their rejection. Her team, the girls' team, would never have treated a boy joining their practice as she had been treated. Maybe women *are* more sensitive than men, she sighed. On the other hand, there was her father. If the Saint had been on that team, he would have unconditionally welcomed her or any other girl. She laughed quietly to herself. The Saint would accept anyone. He simply could not compete. She could even imagine his throwing the ball to the opposing team because they were losing and he wouldn't want them to feel bad—especially if they were visitors. Well, the Saint might never be able to make it in the real world, she thought, but who says the real world is so great, anyway? It sure didn't feel great, right now. She should be jumping for joy, celebrating. She had just done a fabulous job, but here she was, standing in the shower, all alone, with no one to even pat her on the back, throw an arm around her, or tell her how well she had done.

Cass rinsed off, toweled her body and long hair, partially dried it with a dryer, then got out her clothes. She took a long time dressing. She didn't want to run into any of the boys on their way out. As she laced up her Reeboks, she decided to stop by Coach Morris's office to thank her for showing up, for giving her the support she needed—and also for that pat on the back she longed to feel. Hell, what's the use of winning, she thought, if there's no one to share the victory with? If there's no way to release that staccato beat of exhilaration fluttering in your chest, it just turns in on you, and that delicate feeling, so hard to hang on to, gradually slides into sadness.

Cass picked up her gym bag and headed out the door, feeling a little better, anticipating a big hug from Coach Morris, who was not afraid to express her enthusiasm physically with a hug, an arm around your shoulder, or a pat on the back. She had seen Turner slap his boys on the back and punch them playfully, too, but she knew he would never touch her.

"Like hell, she will!" Cass heard Turner yell as she turned the corner next to Coach Morris's office. She stopped in her tracks and stood perfectly still.

"Come on, Barney," Coach Morris coaxed. "She's a better player right now than half the guys on your team. After she works out with you for a month, she'll be ready to start."

"No," Coach Turner said adamantly. "Absolutely not."

"You could do wonders with her," Carla Morris said

enthusiastically. "I mean, look what I've done, and I'm not half as good a coach as you are."

"That's true," Turner agreed.

"Then give it a try," Coach Morris begged.

"Carla," Barney Turner said, softening up a little. "I can't let a broad play on my team."

"Barney, she's not a broad. She's a damn good player. Now you said you'd give her a chance, and—"

"And I gave her a chance," Turner said, interrupting Coach Morris.

"And she was a knockout."

"That doesn't mean I have to let her play with the team. I said I'd give her a chance to work out with us. I didn't say anything about letting her play in a regular game. Geez, are you kidding, Carla? Geez! I can't even imagine a thing like that."

"Why not?" Coach Morris asked innocently.

"Why not? What do you mean, 'Why not?'"

"I mean, why not, what do you think I mean?" Carla Morris said, emphatically.

"You trying to confuse me or something?" Turner asked, getting angry.

Cass could hardly believe that this guy could figure out the complicated moves he introduced to his team, let alone explain how to execute them.

"Barney," Coach Morris said quietly, softening him up again, "Barney, listen. You've taken the championship three seasons in a row. No school in California has won the championship four times. Everybody's going to be watching us—the whole state and every scout from every decent school from here to New York."

"Exactly," Coach Turner said triumphantly.

"You could use Carothers to your advantage. Show everybody what a forward-looking person you are.

Show them that you're a man who can look to the future, who isn't afraid of taking chances."

"Yeah, well, there's one thing I am afraid of," Coach Turner said disdainfully. "If I had a female on my team, every coach in the league would laugh his head off at the Wildcats. I can hear 'em now. 'When you gonna change your name to Wildkittys, or Wildpu—?' Excuse me. I got a little carried away, but you get the point, I'm sure."

"Sure, I get the point, but I never thought you'd be the type who couldn't stand up to some stupid remarks from jealous colleagues, who were too macho and too backward to take the kinds of chances you take, the kinds of chances I see you taking all the time with your boys, the kinds of chances which make your team a championship team. Letting Carothers play with you is just an extension of what you already do, anyway," Coach Morris said, ending her little speech with a flourish. Cass had to give her credit. She had a real way with words. She smiled. She had never heard Coach Morris manipulate anyone the way she was working Turner over.

"Wellllll," Turner said.

Cass held her breath.

"Well?" Coach Morris asked, pushing him.

"Nah," he said slowly, as if he weren't quite convinced that was the right answer. "Nah," he repeated. "There would be too many problems."

"No, there wouldn't," Coach Morris said quickly. "At least none that couldn't be easily solved."

"Carla, listen. I know what you're saying, and maybe you're right to a certain extent, but being on a team is more than just playing with a group of men. It's part of something bigger than that. It's the comradeship. It's that special feeling you get dressing together in the locker room, telling jokes and stuff."

Cass leaned against the wall. She had to admit Coach Turner had a point there. She would miss the camaraderie in the dressing room—the jokes and fooling around, all the laughs, and the complaints about the other teams and the referees. She would miss the look on Coach Morris's face when, as they were getting out of the showers, she'd come in to tell them how terrific they were, even when they lost. Yeah. He had a point all right, but it wasn't going to keep her off that team if she could help it.

"Barney, I know what you mean," Coach Morris said, mirroring Cass's thoughts. "But she can tell a joke like the rest of them. Okay, so she doesn't get in the showers with the team," Coach Morris laughed. "At least we hope she doesn't. Anyway—"

"What do you mean, 'hope she doesn't'?" Turner interrupted. "She got some problems there?"

"*Nooooo*. Hell, no," Carla Morris laughed. "I was just trying to be funny."

"Oh," Barney Turner said, laughing a little uncomfortably, "that is funny."

"Yeah. Anyway, what I was trying to say was that Cass can take care of herself. She always has. Sure, she'll miss out on some of the joking around and some of the other stuff, but I think it would be worth it to her in the long run. Now, do me a favor, Barney. Do yourself a favor and tell the girl she can play on your team."

"I'm sorry, Carla. I really am." Turner said it as if he really meant it.

Cass sank to the floor.

"I'm going to have to say no. It just wouldn't be good for morale. I can't do this to the rest of the team. It just wouldn't be fair."

"Fair?" Coach Morris asked, her voice suddenly tense. "I've tried to be reasonable, tried to present our case fairly to you, tried to help you understand how important this decision is, but, much as I hate to do this, I'm going to have to explain to you about fair. Would it be fair to say that you desperately need a new basketball court and that you expect to get one next season? Would that be a fair assumption?"

"Hell, yes, we need that floor, and I'm going to get it," Barney Turner said, raising his voice.

"How much is it worth?"

"What are you trying to do, bribe me? I'm ashamed of you, Carla," Coach Turner said, almost laughing.

"I'd never do a thing like that Barney, dear," Carla Morris said sweetly. "I'd never be able to come up with the money, but I just thought I should remind you—because I have a great deal of respect for you, and because I, too, would love to see you get that floor—that all new equipment, requisitions, and additions have to be okayed by our principal."

"So?"

"So, Barbara Carney would love to see a woman on the basketball team. If I remember correctly, she played some basketball in college, herself. I heard her mention, at the faculty meeting, that we might not be able to afford new equipment because of the tax-bond failure last year, and she knew you'd be as disappointed as she was if you couldn't get that floor. But what can she do? She has to cut back someplace. On the other hand, a coach who showed initiative, concern for *all* the students, not just—"

Cass picked up her books and gym bag, and slipped quietly back down the hallway and through the door.

CHAPTER FIVE

"Go, boy," Cass begged as she tried to coax Willie Boy to start. "It isn't raining, yet." She sighed. "You usually wait till it rains to stall on me." She pumped the gas pedal furiously, and the engine caught. "Good boy." She checked her watch as she slid into reverse and ripped out of the driveway. Twenty minutes. She could make it to school on time if there wasn't too much traffic. She'd better make it to school on time, she thought. She'd been late three days in a row. The fourth time, the dean calls home. Very funny, she laughed to herself. Sky would just tell him she didn't believe in external time clocks. "Everybody has to listen to his own body," she'd say. "If Cass gets up late, that must mean that her body is telling her something." It was telling her something right now, all right. It was telling her she was damn hungry. She hadn't had time for breakfast.

The bell rang as Cass slipped into English class and looked around. The teacher wasn't there, yet. Good deal. She'd have a few minutes to talk to Kathy. "So, how'd it go last night?" she asked Kathy, sliding into the seat next to her.

"We missed you, hot shot," Kathy answered. "How's it going for you?"

"Well, I'm kind of nervous," Cass said. "Maybe I should have stayed with you guys," she added nostalgically.

"Hell, no, you made the right choice. It'll get easier," Kathy whispered. "They just have to get used to you."

"I don't think they like me," Cass said, looking over at Julio, who was huddled over his English book.

"Their loss," Kathy said casually, making a face at Jackson and Weiner.

Cass started to laugh as Teri Redman walked into the classroom. The rest of the class continued chattering away, totally unaware of her presence, which was understandable since she didn't look much older than they did, and to top it off, she was only five feet high. She tried to counter this by wearing high-heeled shoes and boots, but they all teased her unmercifully about her height, anyway. Cass always felt rather silly asking her for help, since Teri only came up to about her knees, and she felt she was the one who should be helping Teri out, instead, but Teri was a good guy. She was honest. She was a hard grader, but she was fair. She didn't take anything from anyone, but she had a good sense of humor. She could relate to kids. She was one of the few adults, besides Coach Morris, who really understood them.

"Anyone know who Oedipus Rex was?" Teri said, banging on her desk for attention.

"I think he was in *Superman III*," Jackson yelled out from the back of the room, as everyone took his/her seat.

"Oedipus Rex was a very complex man," Teri Redman said, raising her eyebrows and smiling slightly as she cocked her head to one side. She always did this when she told a joke. In case you didn't get it, it was her way of announcing that you should laugh, anyway.

"Bad joke," Weiner groaned, "Try again, miniperson."

"Okay. When I said Oedipus was a complex man, I was making a pun."

Everyone groaned simultaneously.

"Oh, all right. I see you know what puns are. But they can be an interesting way to practice using the language. We all talk easily. English is our native tongue. We don't think twice about it, until we have to write it down; then we suddenly realize there are several spellings for the same word, and words can sound the same and mean something entirely different. These words are called homonyms."

"For example?" Kathy asked.

"Okay, how can you tell a male chromosome from a female chromosome?" Teri asked.

"This is English, not science," Weiner whined.

"You can tell a male chromosome from a female chromosome by pulling down his genes. G-E-N-E-S," Teri said, laughing. "That's an example of a homonym."

The class broke up laughing. Cass looked over at Julio, who was trying not to look puzzled. It was obvious that although he had been born in California, he had not learned to speak English until he started school. He still missed some of the subtler phrases and jokes people made, though he would never admit that. Cass had noticed this for the first time last year, however, and she secretly watched him when she felt he might feel uncomfortable about not recognizing a word. She held her breath for him until he got past the discomfort and uncertainty. She saw him slip his hand into his book bag and pull out a dictionary. He flipped through the pages quickly, stopped, read for a moment, then smiled broadly. Cass let out her breath. Boy, she admired that kid.

Miss Redman spotted Julio's dictionary just as he was putting it back into his bag. "Wait a minute," she cried. Julio froze and slumped into his chair. Cass knew he had not wanted to be caught looking up a word. Only geeks looked up words in the dictionary.

"Hold up that dictionary, Julio," she commanded. Julio just sat there, but Miss Redman went on, oblivious. "I want all of you to carry one of those around with you. Understand! You're going to need it for *Oedipus*." Loud groans. "Come on," Teri coaxed. "You're gonna love *Oedipus*. It has everything a modern bestseller has—murder, incest, intrigue."

"I'm not sure my mother will let me read it, then, Miss Redman," Jackson said. "She's always telling me to lay off those kinds of books and read something worthwhile."

"*Oedipus* is worthwhile, I assure you," Teri said, laughing.

"Hey, man, this is the first time I ever heard anyone call murder and incest worthwhile. You must be some kind of pervert or something," Tony Raden said, laughing, pretending to be shocked. Teri laughed with him, and so did the rest of the class. Cass glanced over at Julio again. He was smiling uncomfortably and literally squirming in his seat. Cass knew that in his culture, students would never clown around like this with a teacher.

"You're a bit hyperkinetic today, Raden," Miss Redman said when Tony continued laughing long after everyone else had calmed down.

"Good word," Jackson said. "What's it mean?"

"Look it up in the dictionary," Teri said, pointing to Julio's now nonexistent book. It had disappeared minutes ago, into the safety of his book bag.

"But I don't have a dictionary," Fred Jackson said. "My mother doesn't believe in dictionaries. She thinks they inhibit creativity."

"Well, I *do* believe in dictionaries," Teri said

emphatically, "and I want every one of you to get one and use it!"

The bell rang in the midst of groans and general chaos, and everyone ran for the door. Cass tried to catch up with Julio. She wanted to make small talk of some kind, let him know she understood. She knew that he was an outsider, too. She needed his support on the team. She wanted him to recognize they were more or less in the same boat. She was a woman on a male team, and he was the only Mexican-American. He could pretend all he wanted to that it didn't matter to him, that he was just like any other player; but deep down he must know that he stuck out almost as much as she did. Why couldn't he just smile at her one time, give her some subtle sign of support when she tossed a ball into the basket? Instead, he turned away, as if he couldn't stand to look at her.

"So, what do you think?" Kathy asked as they walked away.

"About what?"

"About what I said," Kathy said pouting. "Wanna work out with us after school for a while?"

"You know I do," Cass said, "but I can't miss a practice with—"

"Yeah, I know," Kathy said, cutting her off. "I just hoped maybe the boys' practice was later than ours, today."

"Come with me, Kathy," Cass begged.

"Where?" Kathy asked, surprised, not understanding what Cass meant.

"To practice after school. I'm scared. Turner hates me. Jackson hates me. Weiner hates me. The whole team hates me."

"You're crazy. They wouldn't let you play on the team if they hated you. You aren't *that* good."

"Thanks," Cass said, smiling slightly. "I guess that was sort of a compliment, wasn't it?"

"More or less."

"Come with me, anyway," Cass said.

"I would," Kathy said, as they walked into their next class, "but I can't. I have practice, too. It's not the major leagues, but it's important to me."

"I know," Cass said as they sat down. "I just thought—oh well."

By the end of the day, Cass had worked herself up into a quiet hysteria. This was the first real practice in which she was officially a member of the team. She knew the boys resented her, felt she was being forced on them, and that it wouldn't be the same with her there. She decided she'd be as cool as possible and try to more or less fade into the game, not try anything fancy, just do what she was told.

She dressed in the locker room and walked slowly out to the court. Turner was standing by the door. Most of the guys were shooting baskets. Cass tried to slip in past Turner, but he called to her. She took a deep breath and turned around to face him.

"I just wanted to tell you, Carothers," he said. "The guys aren't too happy about your being on the team. You know that. But I promised to give you a chance to play with us, and I'm gonna keep my promise. Only thing is, I want you to know that if you change your mind, decide you can't take the heat—well, we'll understand."

"I understand," Cass said, seething. Why did he have to say that? It wasn't as if she didn't already know it, but saying it somehow made it worse.

"Yeah, I promised to give you a chance on the team," he repeated, "but I didn't promise the boys wouldn't give you a hard time, sweetheart."

Cass cringed and started to walk away.

The coach was mumbling to himself. "The broad isn't bad-looking for a broad," he grumbled. "Why doesn't she want to be a model like every other girl?"

"'Cause I'm not a broad," Cass yelled, spinning around to face Coach Turner again. "I'm a woman, and a damn good basketball player, too."

CHAPTER SIX

Cass could feel her face burning as she stomped away from Turner and walked onto the court. Damn him, she thought. And damn the whole team. She was sure they had all overheard the outburst, but they continued playing their little game as if they hadn't listened to a thing, as if they weren't the least bit aware of her or her feelings. They were practicing their sky hooks and jump shots, tossing the ball to each other, yelling, "Watch your right. Watch your left." But they sure had been quiet two minutes ago, she thought, quiet enough to hear every word. Not that she had expected anyone to come to her defense; but they could have shown a little support in some small way, like throwing her the ball when she walked toward them, or calling to her, or just acknowledging her in some way—any way. She looked at Julio doing lay-ups by himself in the opposite court. His back was toward her. She walked over to him. Right now he seemed less menacing to her, maybe because he was more her height, almost an inch shorter than she was, in fact; and even though she was six feet, she was dwarfed by Jackson, Weiner, Raden, and Anderson. "Can I try one?" she asked as casually as possible.

"It's all yours," Julio answered, just as casually, as he tossed her the ball. She smiled at him, but he turned around and walked toward the other players.

Cass shot a few baskets, but watching the ball fly

through the hoop somehow didn't seem all that thrilling, anymore.

Turner blew his whistle and assembled the team for warm-ups. "Okay, guys," he said. "First, let's do a few laps around the floor."

"How many?" Weiner asked, already taking off. His long, long legs seemed to reach to his blond, curly hair. He looked like a Greek god gliding across the floor.

"Fifty laps for the guys, and—ah—thirty for the lady," the coach said, bowing to Cass.

"I'll do the fifty," she said, taking off with the rest of the team.

He's just trying to test you, she told herself as she sped around the court in back of Stevens, trying to pace herself so she wouldn't run out of steam.

You can do it. "Push," she said to herself, her thighs and calves straining. Why was she so tight? she wondered. Fifty laps were nothing to her. Last year, she had run fifty laps easily. She had run seventy laps without really feeling it. But her whole body was tight, right now. She could feel the tension in the back of her neck as it spread through her shoulders. She shook her head slightly from side to side as she ran, hoping to loosen up a little.

There were fourteen men and one female jogging around the court, legs flashing as they sped past the coach, but Cass knew that the one pair of eyes she was most concerned about impressing had never left her. She could feel Turner's steady gaze penetrating her back, right between her shoulder blades, and she involuntarily tightened up again. Her breathing began to come in spurts—shallow, difficult breathing. "From the stomach, not the chest," she whispered to herself. "Relax, just relax," she continued. "This is only the beginning. You can do it. You *can* do it," she repeated to herself over and over again. The breathing became easier. She could feel the tension between her shoulder blades begin to ease up.

Cass came around the fiftieth lap breathing hard, but she could hear the guys in back of her panting just as hard as she was. Good, she thought, let them see I'm no pushover.

"Very nice, young lady," Turner said. "That was very nice, indeed."

Cass tried not to blush. She was so fair that the least hint of embarrassment showed in her face. She knew that not even the tan she acquired in summers could hide her self-conscious glow when she blushed. She'd give anything right now to be as dark as Fred Jackson. His smooth, black skin shone with sweat as he slowly paced the floor; but if Fred ever felt embarrassment, he could sure hide it from anyone else, she thought.

"Give her a hand, boys," she heard the coach add sarcastically.

The team clapped politely, as if it had just sat through a performance of the Juilliard String Quartet during tea with the principal. "Very nice, indeed, young lady," Weiner said, sugary sweetness all but oozing out of his mouth.

Cass's stomach leaped up to her own mouth, and she wanted to gag on the saccharine. Instead, she smiled at Weiner and said, "Glad you liked it. You oughta see what I can do when I try."

Weiner raised his bushy, blond eyebrows but didn't say anything else, although there were a few snickers from the rest of the guys.

"Okay, enough fooling around," Turner yelled. "On your feet for fifty jumping jacks."

Jackson, Weiner, Anderson, and Stevens jumped up first and the rest of the team followed. Cass jumped up with them. She didn't want to appear too anxious, but she didn't want to be the last to get into position, either.

"One, two, three, four," the coach sang out. "Two, two, three, four. Three, two, three, four. Get those arms up in the air, get those legs moving," he yelled as the team jumped higher. "What the hell do you think you're doing? Dancing the waltz or something? This is serious business. Raden, damnit, get your ass in gear. Move. That's better. Higher, Martinez. Reach for it, you candy-ass."

"Geez, Carothers," the coach started to say before he caught himself. "I mean, Miss Carothers, would you mind lifting your arms just a little higher into the air?"

Cass stretched as high as she could. Her arms ached. She brought them down to her sides, slamming them against her hips, glad to drop them down, if only for a moment.

"That's fine, just fine," Turner said, staring at her, his eyes boring through her. Cass began to sweat. "Very fine. Very good—for a girl," the coach added, then he went back to his regular routine. "Higher, damn it. I said higher, Anderson."

Cass glanced at Anderson. He looked pale; his millions of freckles stood out against his pasty white face, but he smiled eagerly when he saw her looking at him. He was tired, she knew, but she also knew he'd never admit it. Hell, she wouldn't admit it, either, but she'd love to just slide down on the floor this very minute, close her eyes, conk out, and forget the whole thing. Why was she abusing herself this way? Abusing her mind as well as her body? "Higher, Miss Carothers," the coach pleaded. "You'll never make it to the championship game."

With a rush of adrenalin, Cass jumped higher. That

was the reason she was abusing her mind and her body, and she couldn't forget it. The championship game. She'd jump from now until tomorrow, if she had to, but she was going to make it to that game—with the team. "Damn right, I am," she said to herself. "I'm going all the way."

Cass reached for the ceiling, her arms high above her head, her legs wide apart at first, then close together, her back and head perfectly straight. A faint smile escaped, as a gurgle of excitement tickled her insides. She could feel a trace—a tiny trace—of that old self-confidence she had parked at the door.

"Lay-ups," Turner shouted, blowing his whistle.

The team lined up with Weiner, Jackson, and Stevens in the first three positions, as always. Cass walked to the end of the line and stood in place, wishing she had a ball in her hands to dribble while she waited her turn.

Just as Weiner was about to shoot, he turned around and looked at Cass. "Oh, I'm so sorry," he said, walking back to where she was standing. He stood in front of her. "Ladies first." With an overhand motion, he gently threw her the ball and took her place at the end of the line.

Angrily, she sped across the court, dribbling the ball frantically.

"Carothers," Turner shouted. "What the hell kind of game do you think we're playing here? This is a *boys'* team. Now take the ball down the court under control," he said, scowling. Cass continued dribbling and looked at him. "If you don't mind, that is," he added with a hideously condescending grin. "Like Weiner said, ladies first, Miss Carothers, but try not to take advantage of our consideration."

Cass carefully dribbled the ball several times, then filled the basket with a spectacular shot from the left.

"You're right," she said, grinning. "You're right, Weiner. Some ladies are first."

"Yeah, and what's that supposed to mean?" Weiner
asked, forgetting himself for a moment.

Looking directly at Weiner and then at the coach,
Cass said, "It means that it's not what's in the
J-E-A-N-S that counts, but what's in the G-E-N-E-S,"
and she tossed the ball to Jackson without taking her
eyes off the coach.

"*Whoooo*," Stevens said, laughing. "The girl's
sharp."

"Lady," Cass corrected him.

"Lady," Stevens said with a tinge of respect in his
voice.

"On the ground for pushups," Turner said, annoyed.
"Fifty of them, and you all know why."

Obviously, she had gone too far, Cass realized. It
was fine to take a stand and show the team she could
dish it out as well as take it, but she shouldn't have
included the coach in her look of triumph. He resented
her enough as it was, and he was the one who decided
who would play and who would sit on the bench. It
wasn't enough to just make the team; it was even more
important to go the distance in a real game.

"Five, six, seven, eight," the coach droned on as
the team lay on their stomachs, pushing their arms off
the ground. Cass's arms were shaking, and her stomach
muscles ached. She couldn't do fifty pushups.

"A little control there, Carothers," the coach said,
gloating.

Julio coughed self-consciously, as if he were embarrassed by the coach's sarcasm.

Out of the corner of her eye, she saw Weiner wink
at her as if he silently supported her. She couldn't
believe it.

Still, her arms shook. "Fifteen, sixteen," the coach shouted. "Control, Carothers. Keep control."

"Not exactly fair," Jackson said under his breath as he pressed the floor on the other side of her.

Cass collapsed. She couldn't go on, no matter what. Not today.

"Okay, Carothers," the coach sighed. "While the rest of the team is completing their pushups and taking a break, you run the center stairs."

Cass could barely pick herself up off the ground. Everything ached now, not only her arms and stomach. Instead of walking to the stairs, however, she ran toward them, as if she was anxious to get there; and, in fact, in a sense, she was, because even though she felt raw with tiredness, she knew she could run the stairs. She could push herself, and she could make it. The stairs were difficult, but right now, the pushups were impossible.

When Cass finished, the rest of the team were taking a break. As soon as she jumped down on the court, however, Turner blew his whistle.

"Okay. Shirts and skins," he shouted. "Same as yesterday. Carothers, you play on Weiner's team— shirts, of course."

"That's okay, coach," Cass said, grinning, now that the ice had been broken ever so slightly with the rest of the team. "I'll play on Stevens' team."

"Skins?" Jackson gasped, amazed.

All eyes were on Cass as she lifted up her shirt. All eyes, except Julio's, that is. Whistling under his breath, probably to drown out the gasps of his teammates, Julio was dribbling across the court.

"Just a minute. Just a minute," Coach Turner shouted, rushing onto the floor, face beet-red, arms flailing in the air, blowing his whistle and trying to talk at the same time. "Just a minute. None of that.

We can't have any of that kind of monkey business around here."

"Really, it's okay," Cass said as she continued pulling off her Wildcats' shirt.

Coach Turner hid his eyes as he continued shouting. The team burst out laughing. When the coach opened his eyes again, Cass was standing in front of him. She had taken off her shirt and was all but waving it at him. The coach paled before he realized Cass was now wearing a red tank top, which had been nicely concealed under her uniform until just the right moment.

Coach Turner coughed to cover up his embarrassment, then blew his whistle for the scrimmage to begin.

"I wish you'd learn some control, Carothers," Cass said to herself, as she followed Stevens onto the court.

CHAPTER SEVEN

"I don't get what Miss Redman meant about a different Creon," Jackson said to Cass before English class. "Do you?"

"Yeah, I think so," Cass answered. "Remember when we read about Creon in *Oedipus*?"

Jackson nodded his head in the affirmative.

"Well, in *Oedipus*, Creon was cautious, but he was honest and very fair. He was also compassionate."

"Right," Jackson agreed. "I guess he was an okay dude."

"But in *Antigone*, even though the name's the same, that Creon is really cruel and very stubborn. In fact, because of his stubbornness, both Antigone and Creon's son die." Cass paused for a moment, thinking, then she continued. "I guess Creon had a point of sorts, since Antigone did go against his law, and he was the head of state, but Antigone argued that the laws of the land aren't always right. The laws of the gods are more important."

"Cool," Jackson said. "Like sometimes you have to follow your own laws even though it might get you in trouble."

"Not exactly your own laws. More like your own conscience," Cass said.

"I believe that," Jackson said.

"But, I guess, in real life, you have to decide whether

or not it's worth it to break the law, even for something you really believe in."

"Yeah, I know what you mean," Jackson said, suddenly getting a very distant look in his eye.

"Come in, Jackson," Cass said, waving her hand in front of him.

"I was just thinking about the cops picking me up in front of Weiner's house last week," Jackson said slowly.

"Picking you up?" Cass said, shocked. "For what?"

"For living, I guess," Jackson said.

"What do you mean?"

"I took the bus over to Weiner's. It was pretty late, around nine, I guess; anyway, it was dark out. I forgot which house was his, so I was looking around, trying to decide if it was his house or the house next door. I was just standin' there, and this cop comes up in his patrol car, slams on his brakes, hauls me over to the car and spread-eagles me while he frisks me."

"Fred," Cass said, reaching out for him, holding onto his arm instinctively.

"He won't listen to me when I tell him I'm looking for Weiner's house, but Weiner hears the commotion and comes running outside, yelling at the cop to let me go."

"My God," Cass whispered.

"After Weiner identified me, the cop let me turn around. He didn't apologize or nothing. He just said, 'We know you don't belong in this neighborhood, so we were just checking you out.' Weiner said what the cop had done was against the law, but the cop said there was a search and seizure law which allowed him to stop me and search me 'cause I looked suspicious. Suspicious, hell. What he meant was, what was some big, black kid doing on this lily-white street."

"That's terrible, Fred," Cass gasped. She could see the anger welling up all over again.

"I wanted to punch him out. I wanted to choke him right there on the spot, and I probably would have, too, if it hadn't been for Weiner. But Weiner calmed me down and said, if I did anything, the cop would have a reason to drag me in, which was probably what he was looking for in the first place. So I went into the house with him, and he told his mom what happened. She said it was a lousy law when people like me were offended by it, but, by and large, she agreed with it, given the times. That depressed the hell out of me. Somehow it was worse hearing Weiner's mother talk like that than being stopped by the cop."

"I know what you mean," Cass said, thinking her own parents would have really raised a fuss and called the police department to register a complaint against the offending policeman for stopping a guest of theirs because he was black.

"Sometimes laws are lousy," Jackson said, as they walked into the classroom. "Sometimes they need to be tested."

"Yeah," Cass agreed, "but it's all in the timing."

"Okay," Teri Redman said, glancing at her roll book. "Where's Kathy?"

"She's sick," Cass volunteered.

Miss Redman made a mark in her book, and without looking up, said, "Feet off your desk, Weiner. Anyone else absent?"

"Everyone else is here," Weiner said, surprised that Miss Redman had eyes on top of her head.

"Good, let's begin where we left off yesterday, then," Teri Redman said.

The class took out their *Oedipus Cycle* and turned to *Antigone*, which they were now discussing.

"Yesterday, I asked how the Creon in *Antigone* is

different from the Creon in *Oedipus Rex*." Teri looked around the class. "Julio," she said, focusing on him, "tell us about that difference."

Julio squirmed in his seat. He looked very tired, as if he'd been up all night. Obviously, he had not done his homework assignment. In fact, Cass remembered, he had probably not done his assignments in several days, which was not like him. Julio looked down at his book. "I'm sorry," he said, finally. "I don't know."

Cass chewed on her pencil. She wanted to transmit the answer by osmosis. She knew he couldn't stand admitting he didn't know it.

"Cass," Miss Redman said, smiling at her. "You tell us the difference between the Creon in *Oedipus* and in *Antigone*."

Cass stared in front of her. She sat very, very still for a moment, then she said slowly, "I don't know, Miss Redman. "I'm sorry."

Out of the corner of her eye, she could see Jackson looking at her, totally bewildered. Teri Redman raised her eyebrows. Cass knew she was surprised. English was Cass's favorite subject, and she was always prepared for this class. The question was simple enough. She was sure Miss Redman was amazed that she hadn't come up with the answer, but somehow she just couldn't one-up Julio again. She knew he had never forgiven her for grabbing the ball from him during that first practice with the team. Not that he was nasty to her, or anything like that. He was always polite, very polite, but she knew that underneath, he still carried the shame of his teammates' teasing. Cass knew that he was different from the other guys. What was fun to them seemed like ridicule to Julio. She was sorry she had taken the ball away from him, but there wasn't anything she could do about that. It was over and past. She could, however, try not to do it again.

CHAPTER EIGHT

To no one's surprise, Cass sat out the first game of the season. She had tried to edge her way across the bench so she could sit next to Coach Turner in order to remind him she was there. She had thought maybe she could physically zap him one and get him to accidentally let her in there against his will. If she could get close enough, she could give him a whammy, she decided, and she had really concentrated, but it hadn't worked. He had said she wasn't yet seasoned enough. He said to take it easy; she'd probably get in there, sooner or later. Yeah, she sighed, thinking about it now. Probably much later, too late to work her way up to the league finals and eventually the championship game. She had to find a way to get into that game.

Cass showered and changed, even though she had barely worked up a sweat from the warm-ups. Some of the girls were waiting outside the gym with Kathy. They had come to see her play. Luckily, she had warned them she probably wouldn't be in the game much.

When she finished dressing, she turned the lights out in the locker room. Part of the deal for letting her use it during the boys' games was that she would see that everything was in place before she left. The PE department didn't want to hire anyone extra to check out the girls' locker room just for her. As she was about to bolt the door, she remembered that she had left her athletic bag inside on the bench. She didn't bother turning the lights back on because she knew exactly where it was. The light from the hallway was bright enough for her to make her way inside. She picked up the bag and was ready to leave again, when she heard several of the other players coming out of the boys' locker room next door.

"Turner's a shit," she heard someone say. She stood very still, holding her athletic bag close to her chest. "He shoulda let her play—at least at the end when we were winning by so many points, anyway."

She recognized Jackson's voice.

"Yeah, like hell!" someone else said. "Coach is just trying to protect us. Who wants a girl—*excuuuuse* me—a lady on the team, anyway?"

That had to be Stevens, Cass decided. She continued standing, waiting silently. She didn't hear them moving away from the door.

"Come on, Raden," Jackson shouted into the boys' locker room.

That was the reason they were still standing there. They were waiting for Raden, who was always the last one out. If it took her as long as it usually took Raden, she was sure everyone would say it was because she was a girl.

"She's not so bad," another voice chimed in.

"Not so bad?" Cass repeated to herself. "That's an improvement."

"She still has a way to go," said someone else.

"Okay, you guys, ready," Raden said, coming out of the locker room. She heard them amble down the corridor, but before they walked away, she also heard Jackson say, "Hey, she has a pretty good hook shot for a girl, ya know."

Good old Jackson. He had come through for her. She raised her arms in a silent cheer.

Cass locked up quickly and ran out of the gym to

meet her friends. The rest of the team was milling around outside, too. They were all talking, trying to decide where to go for something to eat.

"You guys want to come over to my house? My mom said it was okay," Kathy said.

"That depends, McCleary," Stevens said. "What's to eat at your place?"

"We could order in some pizzas," Kathy suggested. "And we have a bunch of drinks and stuff."

"Sounds good," Jackson said.

"Can you lend me some bread, Raden?" Weiner asked. "I don't get my allowance till tomorrow."

"Your allowance?" Stevens said laughing. "You still get an allowance, Weiner? How cute."

"Just during basketball season," Weiner said defensively.

They piled into several cars and took off for Kathy's house, which wasn't far from school. Cass rolled down her car window and offered a ride to Julio and another kid he had brought with him, but Julio refused, saying he and Miguel would walk. Cass pulled out of the parking lot, but before she turned the corner, she looked in her rearview mirror. Julio and his friend were getting into Weiner's car.

When the pizzas came, Cass heard Julio say something to Miguel in Spanish, then he dug into his pocket and pulled out some cash. He counted it carefully, then threw it on the pile of bills which Kathy was collecting to pay for the food.

"How about some music?" Raden called out. "Put on some music with our meal."

"Just what I was about to do," Kathy said, dancing over to the stereo. "How about Menudo?" she asked, unwrapping a new record.

"When did you get that?" Tony said, jumping up.

"Who's Menudo?" Stevens asked. "I never even heard of him."

"You're missing something," Fred said. He began humming and dancing to a Latin beat. "Menudo is the Jacksons, Latin style." He moved his hips as the record played. "Aw right. Turn it up."

"Oh, God," Stevens said under his breath. "Just what we need."

"You don't like Latin music?" Julio asked as he came up to Stevens and stood smack in front of him. Stevens was four inches taller than Julio, but Julio, with his fiercely dark skin and jet-black hair, looked more menacing.

Cass cringed. Julio was usually quiet at these parties, if he came to them at all. In fact, he was usually very quiet. He never danced with her or with any of her friends, and never said much. He just sort of hung out and talked to the other guys, and went home after an hour or so. Maybe he felt the only reason he got invited to the parties was because he was on the basketball team. Maybe he knew that if he were just another Mexican kid at Samohi, he would be ignored like the other Mexican kids were, except when fights broke out, as they sometimes did, between the Anglos and the Mexicans, over one stupid thing or another. Mostly, though, the Anglos stayed away from the Mexicans. They were afraid of them. However, kids like Stevens weren't afraid of Mexicans; they just hated them.

"What's the matter, Martinez?" Stevens asked, looking down both literally and figuratively at Julio. "Can't a man have his own taste in music? I don't happen to like Latin music. Dig?"

"I *dig*," Julio said, angrily. "I don't care what kind of music you like or don't like, Stevens. It's your attitude that bugs me. Do *you* dig?"

"Don't be so touchy, Martinez," Stevens said cavalierly, as if he couldn't understand what had made Julio so angry.

"I ain't touchy, man," Julio said, moving even closer to Stevens. "I just don't like people who put Mexicans down, is all."

"Hey," Stevens said. "Who said I don't like Mexicans?"

"I did," Julio said, refusing to back down. He glared at Stevens. The rest of the kids stood around helplessly, not quite knowing what to do. Cass wanted to say or do something to break the tension, but she wasn't sure how or what.

Julio reached into his back pocket, keeping his eyes glued to Stevens' face. Cass dug her nails into the palms of her hands. She tried to yell, stop. She tried to move toward Stevens and Julio, but the word got stuck in her throat, and her legs turned to liquid. There wasn't a sound in the room except for Julio's uneven breathing. Everyone else was obviously holding his/her breath, just as Cass was. Cass heard a whimper and momentarily wondered where it had come from. Then she realized it had come from herself.

Julio began to move his hand slowly out of his pocket. Cass's voice leaped up to her throat. "No!" she screamed. She heard someone in back of her and another person beside her gasp, but she couldn't take her eyes from Julio's pocket. Before he could take his hand all the way out of it, however, Jackson put his arm around Julio. "Hey, we all know that Stevens has some problems when it comes to us people of the darker persuasion," he said softly, casually walking Julio away from Stevens. "That's his problem," Jackson added. "He's so uptight, he don't even like soul music, man. Can you imagine anybody not liking soul? I mean—hey—Michael Jackson is cool, but he's a cross-over artist. You gotta dig Jeffrey Osborne to really understand black music."

Cass saw Julio begin to relax. Jackson had come through twice tonight, and Cass understood why. Jackson knew how Julio felt. He knew what it was like to be an outsider, even though black students at school had it a lot better than the Mexicans—especially black athletes. That's why he trusted Cass. That's why he had told her about being stopped by the police. Because she was an outsider, too. How strange, Cass thought. How easy it is to shift positions. Last year, no one would ever have thought of Cass Carothers as an outsider. She was captain of the girls' basketball team. She was a tall, blond, all-American girl. She got good grades in school. She was well-liked by the other kids and by her teachers. Sure, her parents were a little different, but Cass herself had languished in the mainstream and could pass for your average suburban high-school student. Now, suddenly, she was an outsider, just like Jackson and Martinez, because she had chosen to make a leap outside of her group. If Martinez had hung around with the other Mexican students, he wouldn't have had to confront people like Stevens, but he would still be an outsider because the kids at school would make him feel like one. Cass wondered what need Julio had to prove to himself, and she wondered why he had chosen basketball to do it.

Stevens walked over to the table and picked up a piece of pizza. He shoved the whole piece into his mouth, but no one paid much attention.

"Eat up, everybody," Kathy said cheerfully, hoping that everyone would forget about what had just happened. No one moved for a moment, then, nervously, they all attacked the pizza and soft drinks.

Cass took a chance and went over to Julio, who

was still standing with Jackson. Miguel, his friend, was standing there, too, looking slightly confused.

"You played a good game tonight, Julio," Cass said.

"Thanks," Julio answered, not in an unfriendly way, but not in a friendly way, either.

Cass stood there for a moment. She didn't know what else to say. "*Ummm*, I—who's your friend?" she finally asked, smiling at Miguel. Miguel smiled back, although he was clearly having trouble understanding exactly what was being said.

"This is Miguel," Julio said, motioning to him.

Cass waited for more details, but apparently Julio had said all he was going to say about his friend. Cass smiled at Miguel again. "You go to Samohi?" she asked.

"I been here five days," Miguel said, smiling back at her.

"Oh, that's terrific," Cass said enthusiastically. "Where did you come from?" As soon as she asked, she wanted to kick herself. What a stupid question. She could feel the smile freeze on her face. Her teeth hurt. Her lips were stretched from ear to ear. She was sure they all knew how uncomfortable she was. Why had she come over here in the first place? Julio didn't want to talk to her, and this kid standing in front of her obviously didn't understand a word she said.

"Five day," Miguel repeated. "I live with my cousin—" Cass saw Julio shake his head, warning Miguel to stop talking. "Five day," Miguel repeated, still smiling.

"We gotta go," Julio said quickly, almost shoving Miguel to the door.

Cass watched them leave. She couldn't take her eyes off Julio's back pocket, the pocket where his hand had rested just minutes ago, the pocket which had made her heart beat fast and her legs turn to jelly. She stared and stared at it as Julio said, "So long. See you," to Jackson. It was his way of saying thank you, Cass realized, but still, as far as she could tell, Julio couldn't have been hiding even a toothpick in that pocket.

CHAPTER NINE

"No, no—child*ren*—children, not childrens," Cass said patiently.

"But children—is just one," Miguel insisted.

"It should be, but English is a crazy language," Cass said laughing. "There are all kinds of exceptions. As soon as you learn a rule, you have to unlearn it. You're right. Usually, you have to add an "s" to make a plural, but with words like child, you say children when you mean more than one."

"I am never gonna learn this language," Miguel said with a sigh.

"Yes, you are," Cass insisted. "You've only been here two months, and you're doing fantastically. You're an amazing student. If I went to Mexico, I couldn't learn Spanish as quickly as you've picked up English."

She saw Miguel blush, but she knew he was very pleased with his progress. She also knew that he had been studying five and six hours after school, and he held down a job as a dishwasher in a restaurant, as well. She didn't know many Anglos who were that committed to studying.

"Okay, explain me 'was' and 'where' again," Miguel said.

Cass laughed.

"See, I told you I'm stupid. You laugh at me."

"Oh, come on. You're just fishing for more compliments. Besides, I think it's cute."

"It's cute that a girl has to learn me how to speak?"

"Girl—hey—what's the difference—girl, boy, parrot. I'm a friend, not a girl, and I don't learn you how to speak. I teach you how to speak."

"It embarrasses me," Miguel said, frowning.

"But you aren't in Mexico, now. It's okay for a girl to help a guy here. It means they're friends. *Comprende?*"

Miguel burst out laughing. "Your accent, she is terrible," he said.

"See! See!" Cass said, laughing with him. "Look who's making fun of whom, here."

Miguel stopped laughing and blushed even more deeply. His whole face was bronzed with embarrassment. "But I didn't mean—I wasn't making fun—please forgive me, Cass. I—"

"Oh, I'm sorry," Cass laughed. "I'm just teasing. Besides, my Spanish accent *is* terrible. Ask Donna Garcia."

"Okay, as soon as I learn English better, I help you with your Spanish," Miguel said eagerly.

"Deal," Cass said.

"Deal?" Miguel asked.

"Deal means I can sure use the help. I gotta raise that grade before semester break. It's the only thing between me and a good GPA."

"Everything here is initials," Miguel said. "How can I ever learn anything? GPA, CIA, IQ—even LA. I am going crazy."

"So? You want to be different from the rest of us?" Cass asked. She saw Miguel begin to relax a little. She knew it was difficult for him to ask her for help because she was not only an Anglo, she was a girl. She also knew that Miguel, like Julio, was very proud, and he hated to admit that he didn't understand anything. But there was something more important to him than his pride, right now: learning English as quickly and as well as he could. Julio had been helping him, but Julio had his own problems with school work. After staying up half the night helping Miguel, it took him so long to do his own work that he was sleeping through classes.

Then one day, accidentally, Miguel and Cass had both come early to English class to study for a test. Cass helped Miguel with some verb tenses, and their mornings together had become an unspoken ritual. Though neither of them ever made specific arrangements, they both came to school forty-five minutes early every day and met in the English room.

Cass had to get up at the crack of dawn, of course, even before the chickens, sometimes, but it was worth it. She had made a friend, and she noticed that Julio was now able to get through the day without collapsing on his desk.

She thought about Julio a lot. She tried to talk to him occasionally during practice. He was nice, polite, but he always looked as if he couldn't wait to get away from her. Sometimes she chastised herself for helping Miguel, telling herself that it wasn't Miguel she cared about, he was just a way to get to Julio. But every time she knocked at Julio's door, he'd look out as if to say, I see you, then he'd lock up the windows of his soul even more tightly than before.

"Miguel," she said, without looking at him directly. "Does Julio ever ask you why you come to school so early every morning?"

"No. I just tell him I go to study, that's all. I tell him one time, and he never ask me again, so I don't say anything else," Miguel said a little uncomfortably.

"I guess you never told him we were friends, then," she said.

· "Not exactly," Miguel answered, opening and closing his book.

"Well, did you say anything about me?"

"Well, actually—" Miguel took a deep breath. "Actually, I didn't say nothing."

"You mean he doesn't know we work together."

"No—not exactly."

"Well, how come, Miguel?" Cass demanded. "Are you embarrassed to be my friend, or something?"

Miguel was squirming. It was obvious that he didn't want to say anything. He hemmed and hawed.

"Never mind," Cass said, getting up, obviously annoyed. "You have to be so macho, don't you?" she said under her breath.

"But you don't understand," Miguel said, pleading with her. "It's not me who's macho—I'm not macho." He started to laugh. "That's why my parents sent me to live with Julio's family. I hate to fight. I try to stop fights. I was always getting beaten up. I hate anything—ah—physical. Is that right? Physical?"

Cass nodded, still not understanding what Miguel was trying to tell her.

"I like to read books. I spend my time in the church in Mexico, not because I believe so much, but because they have many books in there. My parents say I'm crazy. They are very much embarrassed because of me, but I am their son, so they help me get the money to come to the United States to study."

"Oh, Miguel," Cass said, smiling at him. "You are such a funny, wonderful guy." She wanted to give him a hug, but she didn't think that would be appropriate. Even if he weren't macho, he was still Mexican, and there was a limit to what a person could assimilate in a few months.

"You are my best friend, here," Miguel said, slowly. "I am sorry my other best friend doesn't—" He suddenly stopped himself. He had obviously not meant to say what he had just said.

"Your other best friend doesn't what?" Cass asked, frowning. She had a pretty good idea of what Miguel was going to say, but some masochistic little monster inside of her kept egging her on, anyway.

"I don't tell Julio that we work together because he said to me one time, you don't like him, and he has some crazy, bad feelings about you, too. I don't understand why. He didn't tell me anything more. When I ask him again, he says, forget it. So I try to forget it." Miguel looked away from Cass. She knew he felt bad about telling her Julio didn't like her, but he had no idea how bad it made her feel.

"But Julio's a good person, I think," Miguel said. "I wish you would like him, so we could be friends. All of us together."

"Okay, let's just forget it," Cass said, "and I guess we'd better continue to keep it quiet about my—our work. No use getting old Julio upset over nothing."

Cass was glad the other kids had begun to float into the room. She felt like crying. Miguel hadn't told her anything she didn't know, but she had hoped that, by some small miracle, she was wrong, that Julio was just shy, and that eventually he'd come around. But while all the rest of the guys on the team had made friends with her, Julio had held out, refusing to acknowledge her in any way, except when she spoke directly to him. He obviously still carried a grudge because of that stupid first day when she had grabbed the ball away from him.

Teri Redman came in, carrying a bunch of papers. She stopped at Miguel's desk to tell him what a terrific job he had done on his paper, and Miguel beamed. Cass looked hers over, noting the comments, and saw

Julio come in and take his seat, after nodding to Jackson and Miguel.

When the bell rang, Cass made no move to get up. She didn't want to reach the door at the same time Julio did, and she suddenly felt very awkward around Miguel while Julio was in the room.

She brooded all day about what Miguel had said, trying to reconstruct his exact words in her mind; but no matter how she repeated them, the meaning remained the same. Julio hated her.

She was shoving her books in her locker after school, before heading down to practice, when Miguel came over to her.

"All day I was thinking about what we were talking about," he said.

Cass's heart began to beat wildly. Maybe he was going to tell her he had misunderstood Julio and that he realized it when he told Julio what he had said, and Julio had laughed at him, saying he was crazy and that Cass was a good kid. Maybe Julio had even said he kind of liked her.

"What were you thinking?" Cass asked anxiously.

"Well, it is hard for me to admit, but I didn't tell the truth, exactly. I mean—I am not macho, in the normal sense, but I got to admit I do feel funny for a girl to help me with my studies, even if you are a basketball-playing girl," Miguel said, obviously proud of himself for being so utterly American in his openness.

Cass, however, was bitterly disappointed. So, big deal. He admits it's hard for him to get help from a girl. Big, stupid deal. That was not what she had wanted to hear, and right now, it wasn't even anything she was the least bit interested in knowing.

"Fine, fine," she said, brushing Miguel off and grabbing her jacket.

"You are angry with me," Miguel said. "I can see it."

"I'm not angry," Cass said brusquely, looking at her watch. "I'm late."

"I shouldn't have told you," Miguel lamented.

"It's okay. Forget it," she said, walking away.

"But we are friends," Miguel cried, following her, "and so I want to tell you the truth, even if it makes me look bad. It's sort of admitting being macho means I am not macho," he said, very pleased with his discovery.

By now Cass was in a foul mood. She wanted to tell this character just to shove it and leave her alone. How did she get herself into this stupid situation in the first place? More important, why? She stopped and bent down over the water fountain. She remembered why. Well, she thought, taking a long drink, more to cool off than because she was thirsty, it's obvious I'm never gonna make an impression on Julio—except a bad one—so why don't I just dump this guy Miguel right here and now? Who needs to get up at six o'clock every day to help some foreigner, anyway?

She stood up and was about to say something nasty to Miguel, when she saw the hurt look in his eyes. He had offered her his hand, and rather than shaking it, she had bitten him, instead.

"Hey," she said, giving him a punch in the arm, like one of the boys. "I understand. I got an idea. Don't think of me as a girl basketball player who's helping you out. Just think of me as a guy on Julio's team."

"You bet," he said, returning her punch. "Only you don't look like any guys I ever saw."

"Hey, go do your homework. I'll see you in the morning," Cass said, smiling at Miguel.

"Oh, you gonna come to school early?" Miguel asked, as if he was surprised by the information.

"Might," she yelled, running down the hall.

Cass glanced at her watch as she suited up. Oh, God, she thought, I'm going to be late again. Oh, hell, it was worth it, she countered to herself. She was almost out of breath when she ran into the gym. The rest of the team was already doing lay-ups. She'd have to sneak in there if she could.

She slipped between Jackson and Weiner. Just when she thought she was safe, Turner yelled. "Carothers, out of line, Carothers."

Cass stepped out of line. She waited for the coach to yell at her and really make her day.

"Carothers," he said sweetly. "This is practice. Practice begins at three-thirty—on the nose! What time do you have on your watch?"

Cass checked her Timex. "Three-forty-five," she said softly.

"Oh. That's correct," Turner said sarcastically. "I thought your watch must have been wrong, since this is the second time you've been late to practice this week. One more time, Carothers, and you sit out the next game."

"I'm sorry," Cass said.

"Remember that, Carothers," Turner warned, then he turned to the rest of the team. "Back in line. Let's see some lay-ups, you pansies."

CHAPTER TEN

Willie Boy chugged up the driveway, groaning and puffing. He was like a tired old war-horse who just wanted to stand around eating all day. "I know, I know, Willie Boy," Cass said, running her hand over the dashboard. "You just want to retire and sit in the sun. But I can't put you out to pasture yet. I need you, Willie B. I have to get to school and back, and you're the only one I can depend on." Cass sighed as she reached into the back for her athletic bag. She hoped Willie Boy would make it till after basketball season. She knew he needed a workover: oil change, new filters; and the two back tires looked shot, too, but she didn't have the money for that, right now. All her savings from the summer had gone into clothes and school supplies, entertainment, and incidentals such as gas. Willie Boy had a voracious appetite. She had to fill his empty belly at least once a week. She kept track of the miles she drove, since the gas gauge didn't work. She knew the tank held twenty gallons, and she got ten miles to a gallon—ten miles! Kathy's Honda got twenty or twenty-two. But then, Kathy's father had paid seven thousand dollars for her three-year-old used car, and Cass had bought her old coach for fifteen hundred. And she had paid for it, herself. She was proud of her independence, but right now, she felt like screaming. She wanted someone to take care of her! She was tired of taking care of everyone else.

Cass got out of the car and looked at the sky. It was pretty cloudy, she thought. She rolled up the window. It was time for the rainy season to begin in all its repressed fury. They'd had a few warning showers in November and December, but, like uninvited guests who are adored when they first come, but who wear out their welcome long before they are ready to leave, it was time for those heavenly tears to rain down from the sky and complicate their lives again. Guests like Sky and Saint's friends, Leigh and Tuna Fish, who bicycle down from Berkeley every year, unroll their backpacks and settle in indefinitely, hibernating like bears as they store up fruit and vegetables from Sky's garden, which they cook and can. Invariably, they ask Cass to ship their neatly packed boxes back to Berkeley for them, and conveniently, they always forget to leave her money to do it.

As Cass walked toward the house, the anger she had felt earlier returned. The coach's warning to her hadn't helped her mood any, either, and now, thinking about the Fishes made her furious. Damn, they must owe her about twenty dollars. With that money, she could get an oil change. She hated being taken advantage of, but when she had mentioned it to her mother, Sky had just said, "Oh, Leigh and Tuna are so absent-minded."

Cass turned the doorknob and was about to open the door when she heard Sky's voice. Probably talking to the plants again, she thought, unless the Saint had finished meditating early and had come into the house.

She was about to tiptoe into the living room in order not to disturb Sky's monologue, when she heard a baritone voice, and it wasn't her father's. Oh, no, Cass thought. Either I'm losing it, or the plants are answering her back. She peered into the room. Her heart dropped. There stood Leigh and Big Tuna. And it was winter. They couldn't have ridden down on their bicycles. What were they doing here at this time of year?

"Cass," Big Tuna roared. He rushed across the room and picked her up—no mean trick. At six feet four, he was one of the few men big enough to do it. He lifted her over his head.

"I see you're still in good shape," Cass said. You jerk, she thought. Why do you always have to show off?

"We've been waiting for you," Tuna said, putting her down. I'll bet, Cass thought, so you can ask me for a favor.

"It's so nice to see you," Cass said. "Such a surprise."

"Our next-door neighbor was driving down to LA," Leigh said, "so we hopped a ride with him."

So—found another sucker, Cass thought. "Bet he was glad for the company," she said.

"Sure was," Leigh said, "and we were so glad to see Sky and the Saint—and, of course, you. But, unfortunately, we won't be here very long this time. Just for four days."

"*Awww*," Cass said. "That's too bad. Only four days?" Thank goodness, Cass thought. I can't bear them for even that long.

"Want some juice?" Sky asked Cass, holding out a glass and a big pitcher of orange juice.

"Later," Cass said, "I want to put my stuff down in my room."

Actually, I want to see if they've invaded my inner sanctum, as they did the last time they were here. All of a sudden, the Saint's cabin wasn't good enough for them to pitch their sleeping bags in. All of a sudden, I wind up sleeping in there, instead, she remembered. What a drag that was, she thought, as she trudged toward her room. She hated having to rescue her clothes from her bedroom every night, in case the Fishes were still sleeping when she got up in the morning. They were night people, they told her ever so sweetly, and they just couldn't face the day until at least eleven.

She looked around her room. Good. No sleeping bags in sight. Her bed had never looked so inviting, and she didn't want to give it up to anybody else, right now. She needed that particular comfort and warmth.

As she flopped down on her spread, she wished she could talk to her parents, alone. She wanted to tell them about what was going on at school. She hadn't said much, so far, and when she did try to explain to them what was going on, they didn't know exactly how to react. They just thought that since sports were supposed to be aggressive, you had to expect anything from the brutes who competed. They didn't quite understand that she was taking more abuse than any of the other guys on the team. Sometimes she wished her parents would just be normal and go to school and yell their heads off like Kathy's parents did occasionally.

When she came out of her room, her father, mother, and the Fishes were putting on their coats.

"We're going to walk to the Inn for dinner," Sky said. "There's some soup and a loaf of hot bread on the stove for you, darling." She leaned over and kissed Cass on the cheek. "You don't mind, do you?"

"I guess not," Cass said. Stay, she cried inside. I need to talk to you. Can't you see how upset I am? Can't you see that I have something to say, and I can't say it in front of these Neanderthals? *Mommmmmmmmm!*

She watched as the Saint, Sky, and the Fishes all but waltzed out the door. They are so stupid, she thought. So insensitive. All they ever care about is themselves. Well, they can just pay their own bills from now on. They can just worry about the gas and electricity, themselves. She wasn't going to care. If they didn't care about her, she wouldn't care about them. Let them see what would happen at the end of the month, when they were too blissed-out to write their own checks. She was going to be too busy to do it for them, and she would be too busy to run to the store for whatever stupid thing they needed when they were baking their stupid breads. And, furthermore, she was not going to touch that stupid soup sitting on the stupid stove. Nor was she going to take one bite of that warm bread, even if it was her favorite kind. That would show them. If they were too preoccupied to notice how terrible she felt, the untouched food would certainly clue them in. Then they'd be sorry they hadn't realized how she felt when they rushed through the door like maniacs.

Cass was sitting on the couch, staring out the window, but she wasn't looking at anything, and she was too deep in thought to hear the front door open and close. She felt a hand on her head and jumped a mile into the air.

"I'm sorry. I didn't mean to startle you," Sky said softly. "I thought you heard me come in."

"That's okay," Cass mumbled, her heart still beating fast. "Did you forget something?"

"Sort of," Sky said. "I forgot to ask you what was bothering you. I could tell something was wrong from the minute you walked in the door."

"Nothing's bothering me," Cass said, in such a way that it was clear she wanted her mother to ask her again what was wrong.

"Come on, babe. You can't fool your old mom," Sky said, sitting down on the couch next to Cass.

"Everyone's waiting for you," Cass said.

"I told them to go on ahead. I'm not all that hungry,

anyway, and, besides, my cooking's better than Lorna's," Sky said, smiling.

"It can wait till later," Cass said. "I was just feeling kind of bad about some things at school."

"Well, go on. Tell me."

"You go on," Cass said, smiling slightly. "You are not as good a cook as Lorna, and you haven't seen the Tunas for six months. I'll be here when you get back, and so will my problems."

Old mom was okay, after all, Cass decided, slightly embarrassed about her thoughts just two minutes ago.

Sky put her arms around Cass and gave her a hug, a long one, which reached all the way down to her soul. Well, I don't believe in all this hugging stuff, Cass said to herself, but sometimes it sure does feel good. Hell, it feels terrific, she thought, hugging her mother back.

"And if you want to get into a good place while we're gone," Sky said, as she walked to the door, "try meditating."

Cass smiled. Well, she was terrific, her mom, but they didn't call her Sky for nothing. Much as she loved her, her mother just about always had her head in the clouds.

CHAPTER ELEVEN

"Hey, there she is," Cass heard someone say as she walked into math class. She had had trouble getting Willie Boy to wake up, so she had missed first-period English and was just in time for second-period math. She saw all heads turn in her direction; then, everyone clapped. Miguel, she noticed, clapped the hardest. She winked at him.

"Great job, Carothers," Tony Raden said. "It's about time Coach Turner took you off the bench for more than two minutes at a time, right, Coach?" he added, teasing Coach Turner, who stood at his desk letting his sunshine spread through the classroom. His team had done a great job the night before, and he was proud of them. He was proud of *all* of them, including Cass.

"I was saving her, Raden," the coach said. "You got to have strategy to play good basketball. You save some of your best players, then send 'em in when the opposing team thinks they've psyched you out. It confuses the hell out of them, especially if you send in a girl."

The whole class laughed, including Cass. While the coach's statement might not have been exactly true, and while she was more than a little insulted by the comment, Cass was willing to buy it, anyway, now that she had had a chance to show her stuff. She had finally been able to prove that she could really play basketball, even on the boys' team.

"So, when's the first game of the league play-offs?" Kathy asked.

"Friday night. Fri-day night! Right here at Samohi," Coach Turner said, "and I expect every last one of you to be sitting right here in the bleachers ready for some action."

"Do we get extra credit if we come?" Nancy Salkin asked.

"No, but you get points taken off if you don't come," Turner said. "And some of you can't afford that," he added only half jokingly.

There were snickers of recognition all around the room, but Turner's threat was taken in good spirit. Everyone was obviously in an up mood. No one was actually sitting at his/her desk. Kathy was perched on the coach's desk. Miguel was doing his English homework on the floor at the back of the room. Julio was sitting on top of his desk as were most of the other students. There was a party atmosphere in the room.

"So, what are the chances of taking the league?" Joey asked, hoping to get the coach really going so they'd use up the whole period, like they usually did after they won a game. After the Wildcats lost, however, everyone knew it was down to basics, and fast: books open as soon as the bell rang, and probably a pop quiz. When they lost, the whole math class reviewed their assignments before coming to class the next day. However, they had won last night, and everyone had partied. No one was prepared for class, today.

"What are the chances of taking the league tournament?" the coach repeated with a frown. "No chance," he said. "No chance of *losing*!"

Everyone clapped again.

"How can we lose with Martinez, Jackson, Raden, Anderson, Carothers,—" he boasted.

"Let's hear it for the team," Joey said.

"Anybody have anything to eat?" Kathy asked in the spirit of openness engendered by Turner's good mood.

"You're always hungry," Cass said.

"Hey, I didn't even have time for juice this morning," Kathy said, defensively.

"Let's go out for breakfast," Joey said, getting up.

Most of the class got up to follow Joey to the door and were about to dash out when the coach realized what was going on. Suddenly, he banged on his desk. Everyone looked up startled. Coach Turner had taken off his shoe and was whacking the desk with it. "I know what you're doing," he shouted at them.

"We were just kidding," Kathy said quickly, as she walked to her own desk. "We weren't really gonna leave."

The rest of the class returned to their seats and sat down. Only Joey stayed at the door, unsure whether he was willing to give up the idea of going out for breakfast in the middle of math class. The notion appealed to him tremendously. He looked at the door. He looked at the coach. Coach Turner was scowling at him. Joey made his decision and began to walk back toward his desk.

"Where are you going, Rubin?" the coach demanded.

"To my desk," Joey said, rather sheepishly.

"Too bad," the coach said seriously. "I could have used a cup of coffee."

Joey looked at him for a moment, not quite sure he had heard correctly, then he let out a yell. "Aw right," he said. "Doughnuts, juice, what else? I'm taking orders," he yelled as he dashed out the door before the coach changed his mind.

The general buzz in the room continued as everyone waited for Joey to return with the food. Whitman pulled out a deck of cards, and he and Anderson settled in for a game of gin. Kathy and some of the other girls had formed an impromptu singing group and were quietly harmonizing on Lionel Richie's latest hit. A couple of boys joined in with makeshift drums, beating the desks with rulers and pencils.

Cass hummed along as she tried to finish her Spanish homework before class, next period. Now that they were heavily into basketball season, it wasn't easy keeping up with classes, especially when there were midweek games, plus practices. But the party air was infectious, and Cass put down her pencil and joined the other singers.

Hillary, Jamie, Eric, and Sue had already joined the group and were dancing in the aisle. Frank sat in a corner, earphones plugged securely into his head while he swayed to his own internal rhythm. From the way he moved, it was clear that he wasn't tuned into a classical music station.

Julio and Weiner were practicing basketball moves without benefit of a ball or hoop, but that didn't seem to deter them at the moment as they hopped back and forth from foot to foot, swerving around, leaping to the side, moving their arms up and down in an imitation of defensive maneuvers. No one paid much attention to Miguel who had begun his math homework. Suddenly, he raised his hand, but the coach was deep in conversation with Raden about a play from last night's game.

"Excuse me, Mr. Turner," Miguel said patiently, his hand still in the air. "I don't really understand this homework problem."

The coach didn't bother looking up. He continued

his conversation till Raden said, "I think Miguel needs some help with a problem."

"Later, Miguel," Turner said. "This is important."

"It's okay," Tony said. "Help Miguel. We can talk about it at practice."

"Okay, Chavez, what's the problem?"

Miguel walked up to the coach with his paper. The coach had xeroxed several problems for homework and had handed them out in class yesterday. Since none of the rest of the class had bothered doing the assignment, no one had complained of having any difficulty with the problems.

"I think maybe you make a mistake setting up this equation," Miguel said, confused. "I tried to work it out, but I can't come up with the solution the way you said it should be done."

"Let me take a look," the coach said, grabbing Miguel's paper. Cass looked over at them just as the coach was checking out the problem. She could see that he was agitated, but she didn't understand why.

"Chavez," the coach said. "This problem is very simple. If you can't do it, you're missing some basic math."

"But I can do it," Miguel protested. "Only when I do it, I do it a different way. Please show me how to do it your way to come up with the answer you got," Miguel said, sincerely.

"I don't have time for this kind of nonsense," the coach said, annoyed. "It's obvious you should be in remedial math. We can't stop and explain every little detail to you people, Chavez. You come in here and expect me to hold up the whole class just to explain something to you that you should have gotten last week. I can't do that, Chavez."

By this time the entire class had stopped talking and singing and fooling around, and everyone was looking at the coach and Miguel. It was suddenly clear to Cass why the coach was so angry. He had probably made a math error, something he did every once in a while when he was in a hurry. Miguel had probably caught the mistake, and it drove the coach crazy. He hated to admit when he was wrong almost as much as he hated losing a game. Miguel was shaken by the coach's abuse. Trying to contain himself, he just stood there. Julio had stopped his defensive game with Weiner and was watching Miguel very closely.

"I think you just made a mistake, Coach," Miguel said, trying to be helpful.

"And I think you made a mistake, Chavez, coming to the United States and pretending you're just as smart as everyone else here, when you can't even speak the language. You want to learn math— go back to Tijuana to learn it, and learn some English while you're at it, so you and your kind don't have to demand special classes in Spanish when you get here." By this time, the coach was out of control. "Raise our damn taxes, is all you people know how to do," he added under his breath.

The class was stunned at the coach's performance. He was known to fly off the handle when he felt threatened. Cass had heard him scream and swear at everyone on the team at least once during a practice; but no one had ever heard him make a blatantly racist remark, which embarrassed not only the two Mexicans in the class, but the rest of the class, as well. The music stopped. Even Frank, sensing the tension, had taken his earphones off. The thick, uncomfortable silence was staggering. Miguel stared at the coach, speechless. Julio looked at Turner with pure hatred. He was about to leap to the front of the room. Cass could see that he wanted to say something, but he looked at Miguel first and Miguel quickly put his finger across his lips to silence his cousin. Julio collapsed into a seat. Before Cass could think about what she was doing, she moved forward, hands on hips, eyes narrowed to a slit, nostrils flaring.

"You can't talk like that," she cried, "Even if Miguel can't speak English as well as most of us, he's the best student in this class, damnit! And he doesn't even have to use a calculator."

"Sit down, Carothers," the coach yelled. "And mind your own business."

"This is my business," Cass said beligerently. "It's everybody's business."

"Just who do you think you're talking to?" the coach screamed, completely out of control at this point. Cass could feel the increased tension not only from the muscles in her own body but from everyone around her too. No one moved. No one even blinked. She stared at the thick vein standing out on the coach's neck, then moved her eyes down to his fists which were clenched tightly, his knuckles white. He was shaking slightly and, unlike Cass whose whole face was flaming, he had turned pale. "You're going to find yourself in the principal's office, Carothers," he warned.

"That's fine with me," Cass shot back.

"You're asking for trouble, Carothers," the coach said, seething. A burst of gray clouds covered the sunshine he had spread over the room just minutes before. Everyone knew what the coach meant, but no one dared say a word. They were too shocked. The coach and Cass stood glaring at each other, locked in silent combat, as Joey opened the door and danced into the room with bags of juice, coffee, and dough-nuts.

"Here's Joey," he sang out before he felt the heat in the room and saw the daggers of ice shooting back

and forth between Cass and the coach. He put the stuff
down on his desk and looked around. "Well, anyone
still hungry?" he asked in barely a whisper. There were
a few "yeahs," which broke the tension in the room.
Some of the kids began milling around in the direction
of Joey's desk, picking up doughnuts and pouring paper
cupfuls of orange juice. But it was merely an empty
routine to break the unbearable silence. No one was
hungry, anymore. And not one person could put the
sticky, sickeningly sweet doughnuts, which had
sounded so tantalizing just fifteen minutes ago, into
his/her mouth. People were whispering to one another
in reverent tones, as if they were in church—or at a
funeral. And everyone avoided looking at Miguel, at
Cass, and at the coach. There was a lot of coughing
and throat clearing. No one really knew what to do or
what to say. Finally, after an eternity, the bell rang,
and the class filed out of the room into the open hallway
to breathe.

Cass, who had sunk into her desk, finally picked
up her books and staggered to the door, shaking, but
proud of herself. It must be in the genes, she thought.
She had listened to her parents' stories about marching
on Washington and going down to Alabama and Geor-
gia to work in the civil rights movement after Martin
Luther King was shot, but she had never thought that
she would stand up in a group and demand that the
rights of someone else be protected. She certainly hadn't
planned on doing it, and she probably wouldn't have
done it for a stranger, as her parents had, but Miguel
was no stranger. He was her friend. A good friend.
She couldn't just stand there and let the coach malign
him. She felt as if each of the letters of the words he
had spoken were hot pokers, and they were embla-
zoned forever on Miguel's consciousness. She had to
apply a salve to the burning wound. She had to ease

the pain. She knew that there were many people who would agree with the coach, but she wasn't one of them, and she wanted Miguel and everyone else in the room to understand that. Most of all, she wanted Miguel to remember her words, not the coach's. She needed her friend to realize that the coach was a stupid man. At least he was stupid as far as human relations were concerned. And he was grossly unfair. Suddenly, Cass felt weak. Yes, it was true, she thought, he was unfair, and because she realized that and because she knew what she had done was irrevocable, Cass also knew that by standing up for Miguel, she had put herself on the line with him, not only in math class, which didn't matter all that much, but on the basketball court, as well. She knew it in her gut, and she felt sick to her stomach as she fell into the hallway.

Julio came up to her, still very angry. At least, she would have an ally in Julio. At least, he was finally going to talk to her, she thought. Maybe something good would come of this mess, after all. She smiled heroically, wanting to be humble, wanting to tell him what she did wasn't all that much, though, of course, she knew it was.

"I want to say something to you," Julio whispered fiercely.

"It's okay," Cass said, mistaking his tone for unreleased anger toward the coach.

"No, it is not okay," Julio seethed. "I want you to just keep your mouth shut when it comes to me or to anyone in my family, see? We don't need your help. We got along fine without it so far, and we can get along fine without it now. I see you talking to Miguel. From now on, just leave him alone. Leave me alone. You don't know what you're doing or what you're saying. Understand?"

"No," Cass said, shocked, "I don't understand. I don't understand at all."

"Listen, Carothers," Julio said, standing very close to her. She could smell the clean strong smell of soap emanating from his body. It made her dizzy. "You have a habit of butting in where you have no business being, like on the boys' basketball team. You think you can do whatever you want and say whatever you want. You're so busy acting like a man, you've forgotten how to be a woman, Carothers. Now do you understand?"

Cass stepped back as Julio spat out his last sentence. She clutched her books to her chest, trying to protect herself from the incredibly painful wound which Julio had just inflicted upon her. She wanted to say something to him. She tried to open her mouth, but the words wouldn't come out, and she decided it was just as well, anyway. She had probably said enough for one day. She had probably said enough for a lifetime. I am going to join a convent, she thought, and take a vow of silence, beginning right this minute.

CHAPTER TWELVE

Cass shoved her books into her locker and, standing in front of it, tried to decide whether or not to go to basketball practice. On the one hand, she didn't want to face Coach Turner, but on the other hand, she couldn't afford to let down just before the playoffs. But she felt sick. She felt dizzy. She didn't know if it was because she was nervous about seeing the coach, or because she hadn't eaten since breakfast. She had sat in the cafeteria staring at her sandwich and drink as if they were foreign objects that she didn't know quite what to do with. At Kathy's urging, she had tried to swallow a piece of apple, but she couldn't get it down. I can't go to practice, she decided. I'll never make it through the warm-ups. Grabbing her jacket, she raced toward the parking lot and freedom. Before she got to the door of the alley, however, Miguel ran up to her.

"I can't talk," she said, turning around and retreating in the direction of the gym. "I have to go to practice."

"I'll walk there with you," Miguel said, easing into step with her.

"No," she said, almost rudely. "No," she repeated, a little less angrily.

"Why not?" Miguel asked, refusing to accept her answer.

"I just don't feel like talking is all," she said, walk-

83

ing faster, hoping he wouldn't be able to keep up with her.

"I do," Miguel insisted.

"Miguel," she pleaded. "Just—just leave me alone, okay?"

They were nearing the gym. What she didn't need was another confrontation with Julio, which was exactly what she was headed for if she showed up with Miguel tagging along after her.

"Hey, you think I don't know why you don't want to walk with me?" Miguel asked straight out.

Cass turned to look at him. He looked pretty sick himself, she thought. Well, she didn't blame him. She had been so busy thinking about herself, about how angry the coach was and how absolutely horrible Julio had been to her that she had forgotten about Miguel. She had forgotten why she had spoken up in the first place. She had forgotten how Miguel must feel. Instead, she only felt sorry that she had placed herself in jeopardy when there was so much at stake for her. By sixth period, she had decided that accosting Coach Turner in class had been a stupid thing to do, and she was sorry she had done it. By seventh period, she wanted to take back her words. She would have, if she could have, so no one would remember what a big mouth she had.

"I know what Julio said to you," Miguel continued. "Oh, I don't know the exact words, but I can guess. He probably told you to stay away from me, from us, that we can take care of ourselves. Right?"

"Something like that," Cass said wearily.

"Well, he's right. You should stay away from us," Miguel said.

Cass glared at him. The little bastard. How could he talk to her that way after all she had done for him? For two cents, she'd let him have it. All her parents' talk about nonviolence aside. This was one time when at least a verbal punch in the mouth was a necessity.

"Damn," she whispered, under her breath, and turned to walk away.

"Wait a minute," Miguel said, grabbing her sleeve. "Let me finish. I said, maybe you should stay away from me because I only cause you trouble and pain. Every day, you wake up early to help me with my work, and—"

"I have to come to school, anyway," Cass said, blushing at what she had just been thinking, sorry she had jumped to conclusions again, and also sorry she had put Miguel in this position, making him admit that she helped him, that it wasn't just by accident that they met before school every day.

"I know. I know we play this game," he said. "And I appreciate it, and I know that you know how important it is to me to keep it up, but one thing is even more important," he said slowly. "More important is for you to know that you are my friend, not a girl, not a basketball player, but a friend. I have never had a girl for a friend before, and sometimes I feel ashamed that I have to come to you for help, but when I am smart, I realize how stupid that is. Only now—" He paused, embarrassed to go on. This was the longest speech Miguel had ever made. He looked at Cass and said painfully, "Because of me, you are in trouble."

"Hey, no," Cass said. "It's not because of you. It's because of Coach Turner. *He* was wrong. You didn't do anything."

"Yes, that is my point. I didn't do anything. And neither did Julio," Miguel said.

Oh, God, there I go again, Cass thought. That's not what I meant. That's not what I meant at all, but I'm afraid if I try to explain myself any further, it'll only get worse.

"Listen, Miguel, I'm very proud of what I said today, and I meant every word of it"—Cass started to smile for the first time since math class—"though quite frankly, it all happened so fast I can't even remember exactly what I said."

Miguel reached into his pocket and brought out a mini tape recorder. Cass stared at it in disbelief. "Well," he said laughing, you said—"

"Where? What? I don't understand," Cass stammered.

"I tape all my classes so I can play them at night and hear the material over again, in case I miss something in class. If a teacher goes too fast, and I don't understand, I come home and play the tape, and Julio explains it to me when he comes home from practice."

"Oh, my God. Could we blackmail Turner with this," Cass said jokingly. "Better yet, we could play it over the PA system during assembly next Friday, or we could—" Suddenly, Cass was lost in her fantasy and laughing out loud. "He's such an ass," she said, finally. "I don't know why I let him upset me so much. If he wants to be mad at me, that's his problem, not mine. Right?"

She could see the lines disappear from Miguel's face. He started to laugh with her. "Or we could play this during lunch in the area where most of the Mexican kids eat. They might like to hear what Turner has to say about all of us," Miguel said.

Cass and Miguel were both roaring with laughter, tears running down their faces, not so much because of the fantasies but because they both knew that they weren't going to let what had happened that morning interfere with their friendship. Because they both felt that instead of the incident's breaking up their friendship, it had solidified it.

"They'd kill him," Cass said, dropping her books on the floor, while she held her sides, laughing.

"They could blast him off the campus with Menudo," Miguel said.

"You know something?" Cass said, wiping tears from her eyes. "You're as crazy as I am."

"Maybe crazier," Miguel said.

"Oh, God. Oh, no. I'm late again," Cass said, staring at her watch. She got up from the floor, picked up her books, and raced to the locker room.

"I'll see you in the morning," she yelled as she sped in to change.

Cass ripped off her clothes and hopped into her uniform. She was still laughing quietly to herself. Everything seemed a lot better, though she didn't know exactly why. To hell with the coach. He would just have to forget about what went on this morning—at least during basketball practice. Basketball didn't have anything to do with math. And, besides, he must know he was wrong, she rationalized. He'll probably never even mention it again.

She was humming when she raced out of the locker room onto the court.

"Toss it here," she yelled to Jackson. The team was still milling around. They hadn't begun warm-ups yet, though she was ten minutes late. Good, she thought. I'm safe.

Jackson tossed her the ball, and Cass made a soft throw into the basket. She caught the ball on the rebound and buried another one.

"Not bad, Carothers," Jackson said, as he stole the ball from her, "but you have to keep your eye on the ball, not on the basket."

They both started to laugh, as the coach rounded the corner, blowing his whistle, blasting out everyone's eardrums.

"Okay, Carothers, what do you think this is—a tea party? You don't come waltzing into practice ten minutes late and take over like you own the place."

"Sorry, Coach," Cass said, still in a good mood.

Jackson continued dribbling the ball slowly, keeping his eye on the coach.

"I have a good mind to penalize you for that infraction, Carothers," the coach said. "That's the second time this week you've been late for practice. You're benched for the next game."

"Come on, Coach, lay off," Jackson said. "We weren't ready to start yet, anyway."

"Who's running this team, Jackson? Me or you?" the coach asked angrily.

"You are, Coach," Jackson said, shrugging his shoulders and dribbling to the opposite court to get away from Turner's bad mood.

"Okay, let's get the lead out," Turner yelled. "Three in the hole." Groaning, the guys assembled for the grueling workout.

"Weiner, Jackson, and Carothers," the coach yelled. "Start with you."

Cass was terrified. The coach knew that she couldn't make three baskets working against giants like Weiner and Jackson. This was the one warm-up in which height was more important than anything else. The object of the exercise was to test their responses against two other players, and none of the players could leave the key until he/she made three baskets. Two didn't count. You had to be the first to make three, and in this drill, pushing, hitting, shoving—anything—was fair. Cass knew she couldn't do it, and she knew the coach would inflict some grueling punishment on her. She tried. Jackson made his three baskets almost immediately and was out of the hole, replaced by Anderson, another tall player. Weiner made his three and was replaced by Raden. Cass was still in the hole, and she was wearing down. Raden was replaced by Stevens. Cass stayed in the hole. She made two baskets and jumped up for the third one, but Rubin jumped higher, and his elbow defense threw her off balance. She missed. She fell to the floor, exhausted.

"On your feet, Carothers," the coach yelled. "You're out of shape."

Cass started to tell him it didn't matter what shape she was in, she would never get out of the hole, and he knew it. Instead, she figured she'd just keep her mouth shut for a change and wait to hear what he had in mind for her.

"Run the stairs, Carothers," the coach said, walking away from Cass.

"The middle stairs?" she asked, knowing ahead of time what his answer would be.

"All the stairs, Carothers. All of them. We have to make sure you're in good enough shape to play in Friday night's game, don't we? We don't want to put you in there and have you fall flat on your face, do we?"

"But I—" I can't, she was going to say. I can't run all those stairs, then do the rest of the warm-ups and practice. I can't do that. I doubt if anyone here could.

"But what, Carothers?" the coach asked almost gently.

"Nothing," Cass said, and she headed for the stairs.

"That's the way to control women, right, men?" the coach said, walking back to the foul line. Cass could see Jackson's eyes flashing with anger as she ran down the center stairs. Stevens stopped dribbling the ball and looked at Turner. "Let the broad alone," he said good-naturedly. "She's a good guy."

Cass stopped running, her heart pounding from fear at what the coach would say and from elation that

Stevens, of all people, had stuck up for her. Thump. Thump. Thump. Her heart was about to burst right out of her chest. She held onto it with her left hand as if trying to keep it from leaping out of her body. Coach Turner didn't say a word for a minute, then he whirled around to face Stevens. "I think Carothers needs some company on the stairs," he said slowly.

Stevens walked toward the stairs. He winked at Cass and motioned for her to go on. He'd follow her. The coach called a water break for the rest of the team.

Cass started back up the stairs with renewed energy. It wasn't so lonely, anymore. She had a new ally. She ran smoothly, taking the steps easily. Pretty soon she heard the sound of other feet on the stairs, and the bleachers began to vibrate. She heard breathing all around her, and slowly she turned around. The entire team was running the stairs. Cass thought her heart would burst with happiness. Even Julio was behind her, although he didn't look too happy about it. But who cared? He was there. He was running the stairs with everyone else.

Cass sang loudly in the shower. She didn't care who heard her. Before, when she had showered after practice, she had always been careful not to make any noise. She had wanted to be as inconspicuous as possible, so the boys wouldn't resent her intrusion any more than they already did. Today, however, she sang "You got a Friend," an old Carole King song her mother used to sing to her when she was a little girl. She had a friend, all right. She had fifteen of them.

Coach Turner was waiting for her outside the locker-room door. "Like to talk to you for a minute, Carothers," he said, motioning for her to follow him to his office.

Cass walked down the hall behind him. He ushered

her into his office and closed the door. Cass stood there awkwardly. She didn't know whether to sit down or remain standing. She looked around the room, taking in the trophies, the framed pictures of Wildcat teams from the last twenty-five years or so, the frayed couch, the old scratched-up desk piled high with papers. Her head hurt. Her eyes burned.

"Sit down, Carothers," the coach said politely. Too politely, she thought. The calm before the storm.

"Now, it seems as if the guys on the team feel they have to protect you because you're a girl—"

"Sir, it's not because I'm a girl—"

"They wouldn't put up with your laziness if you were a guy, Carothers, and for the good of the team, I can't put up with it, either."

"Coach, I'm sorry I was late for practice. But it's not that I'm lazy. Really, I'm not. I promise I won't be late again, okay? It's just that there were—ah—special circumstances."

"Let's face it, Carothers, you're the special circumstance. You don't belong on the team. I know it. You know it. So why don't you drop out now, and none of us will be embarrassed at the play-offs."

"I don't understand," Cass said, almost leaping out of her seat. "I played terrific ball, last night. You were proud of me."

"We surprised them, Carothers. You were a novelty. The guys were all watching you, and they forgot to watch the ball. You got great legs, Carothers," he said, winking at her.

Cass was seething. She clenched her jaw so tightly she could hear her teeth grind. Rage filled her chest, and she felt light-headed, nauseated, as if all the little capillaries in her brain cells were exploding and she was being carried off on a wave of anger. She wanted to scream. "I played a great game," she said, barely letting the words escape from between her teeth. "I played a terrific game," she said, the blood rushing to her eyes, her eyeballs beating to the rhythm of her heart.

"Like I said, we surprised them last night. Palos Verdes will be expecting you. I'm sure Coach Rogers will warn them to keep their eyes on the ball, not on your ass."

"You have to let me play," Cass said, interrupting him. "I'm on the team."

"I don't have to do anything," Coach Turner said. "But I will let you sit on the bench with the team, so you won't be embarrassed about quitting. However, if you're late for practice one more time, I'll take that privilege away from you, too. Got that, Carothers?"

"I'm going to report you for harassment," Cass said evenly, her head spinning. She was trying to gain control of herself, trying not to faint right there on the spot, but the floor kept whirling around in circles, and her stomach was jumping up and down to a rhythm of its own. Just let me out of here, and I'll make it, she vowed to some unknown god who seemed to desert her when she needed that god most. Just let me get out of here, she repeated to herself.

To the coach she said again, in a voice which was not really hers, but seemed to belong to someone else, "I'll report you for harassment."

"Will you, now?" he asked, laughing. "Go right ahead. After all, it's my word against yours, and after your performance in class this morning, everyone around school knows what a little hothead you are, and that you have it in for me. Everyone knows you'd like nothing more than to get me in trouble because I'm unsympathetic to your dark-skinned friends from south of the border."

Barely breathing, Cass walked out of the office.

She ran her hand along the wall just to make sure she was still walking in a straight line. She looked down at her feet to make sure she was still touching the ground. She felt numb from her shoulders down. All she could feel was the pain in her neck, the tension, and the incredible blackness in her head. She could barely see.

Tears of anger tried to push themselves out of her eyes, but Cass was too numb to even cry. Like a robot, she walked to her car, opened the door, and got in. She sat there for a moment, then she leaned her head on the steering wheel, hoping to get some comfort from Willie Boy.

"Cass," Miguel said softly. "Cass, don't be scared."

She hadn't even noticed Miguel sitting on the passenger side of the car. She lifted her head and looked over at him.

"I waited to see what happened at practice," he said. "It was—I was afraid that—"

Cass groaned and turned away from Miguel. She leaned further into the steering wheel, her head resting on it. Her shoulders shook, but no sound came out for a long time. Finally, she sat up and looked over at Miguel again.

"He's not gonna let me play," she said softly, "and there's not a damn thing I can do about it."

CHAPTER THIRTEEN

For the first time, Cass was glad to see Tuna and Leigh when she walked into the house. They were a distraction, and that was exactly what she needed. What she didn't need was to burden Sky and Saint with any more of her troubles. She felt like a yo-yo. Up and down. Up and down.

"Cass," Tuna cried, as he stuffed a large piece of goat's cheese into his mouth, "how are you, lady athlete?"

"Great," Cass barked at him, rolling her eyes upward. "Where's Sky and the Saint?"

"Getting ready. We're going to the Inn for a marathon."

"The Inn?" Cass asked, surprised.

"The Saint's guru is in town, and his followers have rented it out for an all-night session."

"Sounds exciting," Cass said, as she opened the refrigerator. She reached in and pulled out an apple, one of the few things left inside. Since Tuna's arrival a few days ago, the refrigerator had become severely depleted. Actually, Piggy would have been a more accurate name for him than Tuna, she thought, as she bit down. Stuffed Piggy would be even better. She could just picture Tuna laid out on a gigantic platter with stuffing oozing out of every orifice, surrounded by neatly sliced slivers of lemon.

"Good?" Tuna asked, eying the apple.

"A little tough," Cass answered, still visualizing the serving platter.

"Want to do a few lay-ups before dinner?" Tuna asked. "I noticed the hoop outside."

"No, thanks," Cass begged off. "I just had a work-out." And a workover, she added to herself.

She went to her room and flopped down on her bed till everyone left for the Inn. Then, when she was alone, Cass settled down with a big bowl of vegetable soup, some carrots, celery, and a small loaf of French bread. She turned on her stereo—full blast—and played the new Police album. They were so fantastic. She couldn't understand how her parents could listen to acid rock yet find it impossible to listen to the incredible subtlety of the Police. They called it noise. Noise? Jimi Hendrix was noisy as hell. Insensitive ear drums must be a sign of middle age, she decided. She couldn't imagine ever not liking the Police, even when she was forty.

By the time the first side was over, Cass felt better—a little better, anyway. Even though the coach had warned her that he wasn't going to put her in the league play-offs, she still had some time to work on him. She knew he was really angry about what had happened in math class that morning, not about anything she had done on the team. She also knew that he realized she was an asset, and, in the long run, she was sure he'd give in and let her play, since winning was more important to him than anything else. She'd just have to be very cool for the next few days, not get in his way, do all her work, and show up for practice on time—or even early. By Friday, maybe he'd forget what he said, she decided, chomping on a carrot.

Cass finished her dinner and turned over the record. She opened her book bag and took out her math book. She began doing her homework. She did the first three problems with ease, but she was totally stuck on the fourth one. She went to the phone and called Kathy.

"Did you do the math homework?" she asked when Kathy answered the phone.

"All but the fourth one," Kathy said.

"Me, too. I can't get it to work out right."

"Hmmm. Neither could Miguel," Kathy said. "I think that was the problem he got stuck on."

Cass groaned.

"So, we'll all get it wrong. So what?" Kathy asked. "It's not worth the aggravation. Just forget it. Turner will have some crazy reason why it works. Just don't say anything about it, okay?"

"I hear you," Cass said. "Believe me, I've done all the talking I'm going to do in that class."

"Did he say anything at practice?" Kathy asked.

"Not about that, but he sure had plenty of other things to talk about."

Cass told Kathy what had happened in the gym and in the coach's office after practice.

"So, what are you gonna do?" Kathy asked, worried.

"I'm gonna find some way to get onto that court," Cass answered, "even if I have to play on the opposing team."

Kathy laughed. "I wouldn't put it past you, Carothers. No one could ever accuse you of not having the guts to try it."

"What time is it?" Cass asked, after she and Kathy had done a final postmortem on the day's events.

"It's only nine," Kathy answered.

"Nine? Hell! I'll never finish my homework. I gotta hang up," Cass said quickly, as she put the phone down and picked up her math book at the same time.

"I'll just work out number four as well as I can.

Show him I gave it a try, at least," she said to herself as she began to analyze the problem again.

It took her another half hour to complete her math homework, then Cass took out the Conrad book they were reading for English class. Yesterday she couldn't imagine anybody's committing the atrocities Kurtz has committed in *Heart of Darkness*. But since this morning, she could envision committing at least one murder. She now understood Kurtz's dark side, and she identified with it. Conrad might be right, she decided. Given the right circumstances, we might all forget the rules of society and make contact with those primal instincts we somehow decided don't exist anymore. Cass knew she was pretty much in touch with her own feelings, even though she didn't always act on them, but she had never realized till today how much she could hate somebody. She had never thought she was capable of such feelings.

Suddenly, Cass sat up. Someone was banging on the front door. She dropped her book and ran to see who it was.

"Who's there?" she called before she unlocked the door.

"It's me," Julio said. "I gotta talk to you."

Surprised, Cass opened the door, and there stood Julio, shivering in a light jacket. The night had turned unexpectedly cold, and it had begun to rain.

"Come on in," she said, opening the door wide.

Before Julio could say anything, Cass began thinking about starting a fire in the fireplace and sitting on the rug in front of it, just talking. It would be nice, very cozy, and very intimate. Julio's showing up was a big surprise. And a very pleasant one. This morning, he was never going to speak to her again. This afternoon he showed his support for her by running the stairs with the other guys, and now, here he was, in her house. Maybe he didn't hate her, after all.

"Is he here?" Julio asked, looking around the room.

"Who?" Cass asked.

"Miguel, of course," Julio said, agitated.

"Why, of course?" Cass asked.

Julio reached into his pocket and brought out a handful of little pieces of paper. He threw them at Cass.

"Hey, what are you doing?" she asked, angry with Julio and angry with herself for letting herself get sucked into her fantasy about him.

"I come home from practice. No Miguel. I look around. I wait for him. No Miguel. Then, at eight o'clock, they call me from his work and ask where he is. He didn't show up. That's not like him. He never missed a day, and he would never go anywhere without telling anybody. I start to get nervous. My mother says that he was home for an hour, maybe around six-thirty, seven, but he left without saying anything to her. I go up to our bedroom. My brothers haven't seen him, either. I look through his book bag. Nothing. I dump out all his books on the bed, and these papers fall all over, these little torn-up papers. I piece them together, and I see it's a note to the coach. A note he's written over and over again, probably until he got all the words right."

"I don't understand," Cass said.

"Damn right you don't," Julio shot back.

"Well, explain it to me, then," she shouted at him.

"He wrote this note to the coach telling him he'll meet him in the parking lot at school at eight o'clock. He says the coach should face him like a man on equal terms."

"Oh, my God," Cass said, sitting down on the floor.

"He must have gone back to school," Julio said.

"To get back at Turner for what he did to him this morning," Cass said.

"To get back at him for what he did to you," Julio corrected her.

"Me?"

"You put yourself on the line for Miguel," Julio explained. "You put yourself on the line because you were too stupid to let well enough alone. Anyway, you did it, and he couldn't let you do that for him and not put himself on the line for you. He knew that the coach would get back at you."

"Oh, no," Cass said, burying her face in her hands. "I made things even worse. It's worse than you think."

"No, it's even worse than you think," Julio said. "Miguel is an *illegale*."

"An *illegale*—an *illegale*—" Cass jumped up. "They'll send him back to Mexico if they catch him."

"Exactly."

"What will happen?"

"He'll have to work to earn the money to pay a coyote to smuggle him over the border again—if he can."

"We have to find him. Did you go to school? Was he in the parking lot? Did you see him?" Cass asked, her words coming out in a jumble.

"I went to school. The parking lot was empty. It was eight-thirty by the time I got there. But the place was swarming with cops. All over. One of them spotted me—after all, I'm a Mexican and that's what they're looking for. I got the hell out of there fast. I wasn't sure they'd take the time to find out I was the wrong Mexican."

"Julio, I'm so sorry," Cass said. She wanted to add something else, but she didn't know what to say.

"That's why Miguel didn't say anything to Turner in math class. That's why he motioned for me not to say anything, either. As hard as it was for him to hear Turner talk like that, he didn't want to make him mad enough to check up on him and find out that he wasn't here legally."

"I understand," Cass said. "It all makes sense, now."

"I'm not sure it makes sense, but, anyway, that's how it is," Julio said, turning toward the door.

"Where are you going?" Cass asked, rushing up to him.

"I'm going to look for Miguel."

"I'll come with you," Cass said running to grab her coat.

"No," Julio said. "You've already done enough."

"I've done too much," Cass wailed, "but it wasn't because I wanted to hurt him—or to hurt you, either. It was because I was stupid. And I'm sorry. I'm sorry for everything, and I want to help you find Miguel. He's my friend, too."

Julio stopped, his hand on the doorknob. He paused to look at Cass, then shrugged his shoulders.

"Okay, come if you want to, but I doubt if we're going to find him in Beverly Hills. It might be a little rough."

Cass followed Julio out of the house. She locked the front door and looked around for a car, but the only one in sight was hers. He must have hitchhiked, she decided quickly. Julio started walking down the road. Should she suggest they take her car, or should she just follow Julio? This was not time for indecision, and there was no time to waste looking for a ride. "Come on," she yelled, jumping into her car. "Here's the keys," she added, handing them to Julio. "You know where we're going, so why don't you drive?"

Julio stood on the driver's side of the car for a moment, then he turned and walked around to the passenger side of the car. "Slide over," he said. "I hate driving other people's cars."

CHAPTER FOURTEEN

Julio leaned heavily against the car door and looked straight ahead. Cass could sense his discomfort. She knew he felt awkward for a lot of reasons, some of which she probably didn't understand and couldn't even guess. She also looked straight ahead until they got to the Pacific Coast Highway. When they were close to the Wilshire exit, she asked him where they should get off. "Keep going," he said, "until we get to Venice. We'll try the restaurant first."

Julio guided Cass to a tiny Mexican restaurant, barely visible from the street. As they got out of the car, she realized that this was definitely not a place which catered to middle-class Anglos who hunted down cheap dives with an ethnic flavor. This was the real thing. She stood next to the car for a moment, wondering if she should venture into the place. Julio hadn't said a word about coming in with him, and she wasn't all that anxious to go, but when he looked back to see if she was coming, she leaned over, locked the door, and ran after him.

Though it was close to ten o'clock by now, the tiny restaurant, with six or seven chairs squeezed around tables for two or four, was completely crowded. There was barely enough space to move around, but that didn't seem to bother anybody at all, not even the waiters, who were trying to make their way through the crowd, balancing trays of hot tacos, tostados, and tortillas, with melted cheese and mole sauce running over them. The conversation was loud and the music was louder—quick-paced, exotic, pulsating. While she had been standing there taking it all in, Julio had somehow disappeared. She was leaning against the doorway, so he couldn't have left the restaurant, but she could see every table, and he wasn't sitting or standing at any of them. Suddenly, she felt absolutely naked standing there by herself. She was about to slip out of the door when someone noticed her and pointed. There as a commotion of chairs being pushed back, laughter, whistling, and invitations in Spanish that she couldn't begin to decipher. She felt as if she were in the middle of a foreign country, in which she had no way of making herself understood. Though she did fairly well in Spanish class, she couldn't remember one word, right now, except *venga*, and "come here" was exactly the opposite of what she wanted to say.

She felt as if she were riding on the giant roller coaster at Magic Mountain, and she was at that peak spot where everyone screamed with fear and exhilaration at the same time. She had never been so scared, but she had never felt so alive, either. She could smell every individual odor in the room—the oil used for frying the tortillas, the pepper, garlic, pork, beef steaming with hot sauce, and the frijoles. She could almost taste the salt rimming the margaritas and the pungent beer being drunk straight out of the Dos Equis bottles. She was blinded by the glare from the bright red plastic tablecloths, and her ears hurt when a busboy wiped off a table by repeatedly sliding a wet rag over the center of it.

There was not one other female in the restaurant, and by now, all eyes were on Cass as she stood rooted to her spot by the door. The room whirled around her as she looked at the dark faces bobbing up in front of her. She couldn't distinguish any singular features except rows of white teeth—large, white teeth, some with gold fillings, others with spaces between them. Lot and lots of white teeth—all moving up and down at different times as if they were entirely separate entities.

One set of teeth moved in her direction and, within a second, stood smack in front of her.

"You wanna dance?" Teeth asked in a heavy Spanish accent.

Cass stared at the teeth.

"Hey, *chaparra*," Teeth said. "If you lookin' for some action, you come to the right place."

Cass stared at Teeth in horror. Everyone in the restaurant laughed.

"I'm sorry," she said finally, realizing she was expected to reply. "I'm waiting for a friend."

"I'll keep you company till he gets here," Teeth said, trying to wedge her onto a makeshift dance floor about an inch in diameter, which had been created for them by moving two chairs back.

Cass tried to protest, but Teeth was swaying, and the others were clapping, as if to encourage the absurd pas de deux between the small, square-shaped dark man in the luridly flowered shirt and the tall, blond young woman.

Just as Cass decided she'd make a run for it, Julio emerged from behind the bar. He had obviously been in the successfully camouflaged kitchen behind a door in back of the bar.

Julio said something sharply to Teeth, grabbed Cass's arm, and maneuvered her out of the restaurant. She could hear raucous laughter as they closed the door, but she didn't care. She had been able to get out of there in one piece—something she wasn't at all sure she could do just a few minutes ago.

She unlocked her door, slid into the car, locked the door again, then unlocked Julio's door. He opened it and slid in without saying anything. Frowning, he sat in the car without looking at Cass. "I'm sorry," she said, though she didn't know quite why she had apologized. *She* hadn't done anything wrong. *They* had scared the hell out of her. Julio should be the one to apologize for leaving her standing there while he ran off.

Julio didn't apologize, nor did he accept her apology. Instead, he turned to her and said almost angrily. "Miguel works in the kitchen with some other *illegales*. When someone disappears, everyone is nervous. Half the people in the place are looking over their shoulders every time they pass an Anglo on the street." Julio paused and sighed, then he continued sadly. "No one's heard from him since yesterday. They think maybe Turner blew the whistle on him, and he got picked up, already." Cass looked at Julio horrified. He tried to smile at her. "We'll check some other places, then we'll check Immigration and Naturalization," he said, trying to sound more cheerful. "That's where they keep the *illegales* till they ship them back across the border."

"Let's get going," Cass said as she turned the key in the ignition.

"Turn around and drive to the corner, then go up two blocks," Julio said. "My aunt lives there. Maybe Miguel got lost in the crowd at her place," he said, wryly.

When they had parked on the narrow street, the wheels on one side of the car extending over the matted-down tree lawn, Cass looked at Julio and said, "Don't leave me alone this time. Okay?"

"Yeah," he answered. "I could see you were a little nervous back there." He laughed softly. "They wouldn't have done anything. It's just that you're—" He looked at her for a moment.

"I'm what?" Cass asked, wondering what he was going to say.

"You're—tall," he said, opening the door and leaping out onto the street.

Cass followed closely behind Julio as he walked up a short narrow path to a very, very tiny old frame house, which was painted in alternating shades of yellow and green and had a bright red door. It should have looked garish, Cass thought, but it didn't. It looked festive. Even before Julio knocked on the door, opened it, and went in, she could hear Mexican music and laughter coming from every room in the house, not the kind of laughter she had heard in the restaurant, but innocent laughter, kids' laughter.

"Tia Rosario," Julio called.

At the sound of his voice, eight or ten kids ran into the room from various places in the house, followed by a heavyset, gray-haired woman, who was obviously Aunt Rosario. The kids ranged from about three to eighteen or nineteen, and they were all squealing, laughing, and talking at the same time, happy to see Julio. The pungent smell of Spanish cooking filled the room, and Aunt Rosario was wiping her hands on a towel. Since it was close to eleven by now, she was probably cooking for tomorrow.

Julio very politely introduced Cass to his aunt and her family, and they, just as politely, acknowledged her presence; but once they acknowledged her, the laughter turned to giggles from the younger kids and shy stares from the older ones. Aunt Rosario good-naturedly prodded Cass to move into the kitchen to "taste something nice."

They all squeezed into the tiny, steaming room, alive with a mixture of odors. One of Julio's cousins opened a beer and offered Cass and Julio a drink, which both of them turned down. "We're in training," Julio explained. "Cass is on my team."

"You kidding?" his cousin Manuela asked. "You a girl, or you a guy with long hair?" She looked closely at Cass, who had on a loose-fitting jacket and no makeup. Well, she could look like a guy, Cass guessed, although she never thought of herself as being very masculine, even though she was an athlete.

"Hey, you crazy, Manuela?" Fernando laughed. "This is definitely a girl. Right?" he added, just to make sure.

"Listen, anybody seen Miguel lately?" Julio asked casually. Fernando and Manuela exchanged glances, and suddenly the room became very quiet.

"Not since Tuesday," Fernando answered. "Why?"

"We're looking for him. I don't know. Maybe he's visiting some kid from his class," Julio said, trying to avoid Aunt Rosario's eyes.

"When was the last time you saw him?" Manuela asked, worried.

"Oh, this afternoon," Julio said, trying to sound as nonchalant as possible.

"So, why are you worrying us?" Fernando said, irritated. "You have to check up on the guy every minute or something?"

"You're right," Julio said, getting up. "He's probably home by now, anyway. We gotta run."

"Not so soon, Julio," Aunt Rosario said.

"We'll come back, Tia Rosario," Julio said, motioning for Cass to follow him.

"Yes," she said, "and bring the tall boy with you."

With that, everyone broke up laughing, and Fernando walked Cass and Julio to the door.

"I'll walk you to the corner," Fernando said, grabbing his jacket.

When they got outside, he whispered to Julio, "You think he's in trouble?"

"Yeah," Julio whispered back.

"What kind of trouble?" Fernando asked, glancing at Cass.

"It's okay," Julio said. "She knows."

"Somebody squeal on him?"

"I'm not sure," Julio said, as they got to the car. "Keep your ears open, okay?"

"Okay," Fernando said, opening the car door. "Where'd you get the wheels?" he asked admiring the car.

"Borrowed them," Julio said, sliding into the driver's seat.

"Not bad," Fernando said, giving the car door a slap.

Cass wanted to tell him to treat Willie Boy more gently, but she decided to let it pass. She got into the passenger side of the car, wondering why Julio had suddenly decided to drive. "Bye," she called to Fernando as he walked back to the house.

"Bye," Fernando called back.

Julio sat staring straight ahead. Cass thought he was probably thinking about what their next move should be. Not wanting to interfere with his concentration, she sat watching him.

When the front door of Aunt Rosario's house slammed shut, Julio looked up, then turned toward the house. He looked at it for a minute, then looked at Cass. "Why am I sitting here?" he asked. "I was thinking for a minute I was getting into my car."

Before Cass could encourage Julio to drive, as long as he was already sitting behind the wheel, he opened the car door, jumped out, ran around to her side of the car, and slid in next to her, forcing her over to the driver's side of the car.

"Let's try the Salsa Club in Hollywood," Julio said. "He likes to go there, sometimes, and he knows all the people who hang out there."

Cass started the car, while Julio sat biting his bottom lip. He was obviously very anxious to get going and check out their next possibility. Out of the corner of her eye, she saw him glance up at the house as they drove away, but she didn't notice him wave good-bye to anyone.

CHAPTER FIFTEEN

The Salsa Club was hot, loud, dark, and smokey. Sensuously bound together, bodies slithered on the floor in erotic dancing, and although Cass was fascinated by the feelings of abandon in the place, she was anxious to move on when they found out that no one at the club had seen Miguel.

They left and walked outside into the dark night, the music still lingering in the air. They headed for the car. It seemed to Cass that they had been looking for Miguel for days. She glanced at her watch. It was almost morning, and there was still no sign of him. No one had seen him. No one had heard from him. Julio spotted a phone booth and slipped in. He deposited twenty cents, smiling hopefully at Cass, then began speaking rapidly in Spanish. After a moment, he hung up and despondently left the phone booth. Though they had kept a vigil throughout the night, no one at Julio's house had heard from Miguel, either.

With heavy hearts, they got into the car once again and, this time, headed for the freeway, which ironically, would take them to the Office of Immigration and Naturalization where illegal aliens were detained. They drove downtown in silence.

Twenty minutes later they left the freeway and looked for Los Angeles Street. "Look for three hundred," Julio said as he strained to find an address.

"There it is," Cass said, as she pulled into a parking

space across the street from a large brick building, which took up nearly a whole block.

She maneuvered the car in easily, since the street was nearly deserted, and turned off the engine. It was five-thirty. She had never been in downtown LA at this hour of the morning. In fact, she had rarely ever been downtown at all. The empty buildings looked forbidding, especially when she peered, her eyes narrowing to see better, into the doorways. Asleep under newspapers, homeless people struggled to keep away the chill and get some peace before the daily descent from the outlying areas, when people with jobs would fill their territory.

She looked over at Julio. He was staring at the building across the street, lost in his own thoughts. "People shouldn't have to live like this," he said, partly to himself. "Afraid to protect themselves, afraid to stand up for what they believe in. One time, my cousin, from my father's side, came here from Mexico. For years he worked like a dog to get here. He saved every penny, and he gave all of it to a guy who shoved him under a load of tomatoes in the false bottom of a truck, along with twenty other people, and drove him close to the border. Then, cold and starving, they made their way, at night, across the mountains. One of them cried out when he slipped and fell, and the coyote raised his gun and told him if he ever did that again, he would kill him. No one talked after that, my cousin said. When they finally crossed the border, they could barely walk, but they were so happy that they had made it, they wanted to scream." Julio sighed. "He came to stay with us, this cousin, and my father got him a job as a gardener, not for very much money, because everyone knew he was illegal. He worked for two years. He saved his money all the time and sent half of it to his family in Mexico. Every week he would go to the bank and send a money order to keep them from starving. Then one day, a guy he worked with said he had a cousin who needed a job. The next day, the immigration officers showed up at our house, and Raphael was gone." Julio snapped his fingers. "Just like that. He was gone. No time to say good-bye. No time to argue. No time to run away."

"What happened to him?"

"Who knows?" Julio answered. "He got shipped back. There was nothing we could do for him. We heard from him for a while. He wrote to say that he was working again, saving money again, that he would be back some day, no matter what. But after a while, I think, he just gave up, and maybe he didn't want to admit that. Anyway, we haven't heard from him for two years or more."

"I'm sorry," Cass said. She meant she was sorry for a lot of things. She was sorry about Raphael, Julio's cousin who was shipped back to Mexico. Maybe he was working, if he could find a job there. Maybe he was sick. Or maybe he was dead by now. She was sorry that Miguel was wandering around someplace, alone and afraid. She was sorry that she had never really understood the terror that so many people have to live with every day in this country, so open for her, so free, so giving—if you're the right color. She was sorry she could never make Julio understand that she could feel his pain and sympathize with him from the depth of her soul, not because she had ever experienced anything like it in her life, but because she felt more vulnerable and more human right now than she had ever felt in her life, and she cared deeply about Miguel, who was also vulnerable and terribly human.

Julio looked at Cass for a long time. She felt her face getting hot. He had never really looked at her before. He had turned away from her when she had looked at him. This time, they sat staring at each other. Neither of them turned away. She would have reached out to him. She wanted to. She wanted him to reach out to her, put his arms around her, let her lay her tired head on his shoulder. She wanted so badly to do that, to feel his leather jacket under her cheek, to smell his skin. But she was afraid to move, to create an unbalance when the world between them was finally coming into focus. She sat quietly on her side of the car, shivering in the early morning cold, and he sat on his side, relaxed with her for the first time. "You really do like him, don't you?" Julio asked softly. It was not really a question. It was more of an affirmation, a signal that he accepted and understood what she felt. Cass knew that she didn't have to answer, that the question was rhetorical.

They both looked across the street as the people, already lined up in front of the immigration office, began pouring into the building. It was six-thirty. The sun was coming up over the distant mountains, but in spite of its splendid beauty as it flooded the peaks, turning grays into blues, Cass and Julio were moved only by their concern for Miguel. They leaped out of the car, dashed across Los Angeles Street and, panting, entered the building. They raced up to an information desk at the same time as a young black woman stepped behind it, signaling that the building was coming alive.

"The holding tank's in the basement," she informed them. She pointed outside. "There's an entrance around the corner. It might be open. It might not open till eight. Most of the offices open at eight. Check. Someone might be there, now, at the reception desk."

"Very funny," Cass said as they ran back out the door. "Reception desk." She knew very well that this building housed people who didn't want to be there. It was a prison for those who had fought against poverty and had survived, only to be thrown into the teeth of a system which could hurl them back again to the dogs of starvation. She knew that California wasn't exactly paved with gold, but most of the illegals had lived better, here. They had, at least, survived with a semblance of dignity. Now that dignity was being stripped from them, and there were no pleas and no prayers that could save them.

They knocked on the door of the Office of Deportation in the basement of the Office of Immigration and Naturalization. Cass shivered. After what seemed like forever, someone opened it. Cass was glad Julio was standing beside her. She was scared. She was also worried that they might want to detain him. She looked over at him. "It's okay," he whispered, "I'm legal."

"Miguel Chavez," Julio said when they stood in front of the reception desk. "Can you tell us if he's here?"

Without looking up at them, the clerk behind the desk nodded. He checked through a long list of names. Then he waved them off. "Not here," he said and went on to his other, more pressing business.

As she walked out of the building, Cass felt drained. Though their worst fears were not confirmed—they had not found Miguel there—she felt humiliated and upset by the whole ordeal. She also felt lucky. And she felt guilty for feeling that way, for being incredibly thankful that by some quirk of fate she had been born several hundred miles north of the border. She paled when she thought what little distance separated her from hardship.

"Go home and get some sleep," Julio said as they got back into the car.

"If I can," she said wearily.

Cass dropped off Julio in front of his house. They said good-bye quietly, without looking at each other,

Cass surrounded by her own silent fears, Julio surrounded by his.

Cass pulled into the driveway at eight o'clock. Her body ached from tiredness. Her eyes burned, and her throat was taut and dry. The muscles in her neck and shoulders were tense and sore, and her legs felt stiff. She was so tired that she felt an emptiness creeping up inside of her, and she longed to lie down in her bed and ease it away.

She unlocked the door and dragged herself into the house. Tuna and Leigh were curled up, sleeping in the living room. Tuna was spread out on the floor with his sleeping bag on top of him, and Leigh was on the couch. Cass couldn't figure out why they were in here instead of in her father's workshop, where they had been sleeping for the past three nights. They probably just passed out as soon as they came in the door, she thought, remembering that they had been out all night, too. She picked her way quietly across the room, carefully trying to avoid stepping on Tuna, which was difficult since he was sprawled across the entrance to her bedroom. Unfortunately, she tripped as she stepped over his feet, and he woke up. "Sorry," she apologized.

"What? What's the matter?" Tuna said, sitting up with a jerk.

"Nothing. Go back to sleep," Cass said.

"What's going on around here?" Tuna asked. "Geez, I'm beginning to think the place is haunted or something."

Cass started to laugh. "Meditation must have gotten to you," she said. "The only spirits around here left and settled further south when California was annexed to the United States."

"Oh, yeah," Tuna said before he closed his eyes again. "Then what was all that noise in your father's cabin?"

"What noise?" Cass asked. "I've never heard any noise in there."

"Well, either the spirits have decided to move back north, or the mice have," Tuna said. "Leigh and I couldn't sleep for a minute with all the noise in there."

"You've been awake for three nights?" Cass asked, amazed at their stamina.

"Three hours," Tuna said, tucking the sleeping bag around him securely and emitting one short snore and two long ones.

"Spirits or mice," Cass said to herself, "why can't they just go to church like normal people?"

Cass didn't even bother undressing. She just unzipped her jacket, pulled her quilt over her, and fell sleep, hoping she wouldn't have any dreams to prolong the nightmare she had just gone through.

CHAPTER SIXTEEN

Cass rolled over and whimpered in her sleep. Voices droned steadily in her ear, and she incorporated them into her dream. Julio's Aunt Rosario, his cousins Fernando and Manuela, and the younger children were in the kitchen dishing up food from the stove. Instead of eating it, however, they formed a single-file procession into the living room and out the front door. Suddenly, they were in a desolate outdoor area in front of a makeshift shrine. There was a statue of Mary and Jesus in back of the altar. It was the young Mary from the famous Michelangelo *Pieta*, but Jesus was sitting straight up, not lying across her lap, and he was just a baby. Julio's family put the food down on the altar. Then they fell to their knees and cried. Finally, they got up and left, and Mary reached out for the food which she fed to her dying baby as church music floated into Cass's consciousness. She stirred. The music was persistent. It wasn't church music, however; it was K-ROQ, and it was two o'clock. Her clock radio had gone off. The smells of food were coming from her own kitchen, not Aunt Rosario's, and the pieta was a picture she had cut out of a recent LA *Times*, which haunted her. It was of an Ethiopian woman and her starving child. She wondered where Miguel was hiding and if he had any food.

She kicked off the covers and rolled out of bed. She

hated sleeping during the day. It just didn't feel the same as nighttime sleep.

She went into the bathroom, brushed her teeth, and showered, even though she knew she'd have to shower again after practice.

She felt a little better when she stopped in the kitchen for something to eat before leaving. The Saint and the Fish were sitting, trance-like, at the table. She wasn't sure if they were meditating or just tired.

"Love child," Saint said.

Uh-oh, Cass thought. When he calls me that, it means trouble.

"Tuna," her father continued, "just mentioned that you came in pretty late last night."

"I just mentioned it," Tuna said defensively. "I didn't squeal on you."

"Actually, it wasn't late last night," Cass said, amused because Saint was trying not to show that he was upset. "It was early this morning."

"You know I trust you implicitly, sweet pea," Saint said earnestly, "but I thought maybe you'd want to tell us if you were going to be out all night."

"Sure," Cass agreed, "but you were at the Inn." She knew the Saint was dying to ask her where she had been, but he was always very careful about invading her privacy. Actually, however, Cass was more than a little pleased to note that her father did, in fact, worry about her, as a "normal" father does.

"Sky and I know that you'd never do anything— ah—"

"Foolish," Tuna chimed in.

"Not foolish," Leigh said. "Silly."

"Not silly," Saint mused. "What I mean is," he said, smiling tightly, "Cass, if you're going to stay out all night, please let us know." He paused for a long moment. "And where were you, anyway?"

"One of the kids at school is in trouble," Cass said, taking some pasta out of the refrigerator. "He needed my help. I'll tell you about it after I get back from practice."

"He okay?" Saint asked, changing his tone.

"I don't know," Cass answered.

"There's a soufflé on the stove," Leigh said, eyeing the cold pasta. "It was fabulous."

"I'd rather eat the pasta," Cass said, wolfing it down. Suddenly, she was famished. The linguine was wonderful, but she stopped eating and sat there for a moment. She remembered her dream, and she knew that she'd never sit down at the table again without thinking about how lucky she was.

She began eating again just as the front doorbell rang.

"That's our ride," Leigh said, walking to the door. "We're off to Berkeley."

"I'm going to sleep all the way back," Tuna said, trying to extricate himself from the table. "I'm telling you, Saint, you'd better check out those mice in your workshop. Those buggers can cause a lot of trouble."

With a final push, Tuna stood up, gave Saint and Cass big bear hugs, and lumbered out of the kitchen.

"Think they're hallucinating?" Cass asked, finishing her pasta.

"Probably," Saint said. "Sometimes strange things happen after intense meditation sessions."

"Yeah," Cass said absentmindedly, getting up from the table. "I gotta run. I can't afford to be late for practice." Her mind was already focused on the basketball court, where they would pick up any last-minute pointers for the second round of the championship game, a week from Saturday. Cass was sure they'd win the play-offs and make it to the final game at the Long Beach Arena.

* * *

Julio was already on the floor when she walked into the gym. Cass caught his eye. He shook his head, no, but made no attempt to talk to her. Jackson waved at her. Stevens yelled, "Hiya, squirt. We missed you in English today."

Blowing his whistle, Coach Turner came in the door. "Okay, we know what we did right in the last game; now let's review once again what we did wrong." He took out his clipboard with pages of notes and drawings of various detailed plays.

Cass knew he remembered every play and wouldn't need to refer to the notes, but he probably figured it made him look more official. "Jackson," he began, "too many personal fouls. Watch your temper and your elbow. The referee has eyes in back of his head."

The coach went on to discuss each play, why it worked and didn't work or could have worked better. Cass relaxed. He seemed to have forgotten about their altercation yesterday. He even joked with her once or twice. "I noticed Carothers's unusual defensive technique. Since Kennedy is three inches taller than she is, and she couldn't get her arms up high enough, she dazzled him with her fancy footwork and confused the hell out of him. He threw the ball to Jackson, once, instead of his own team." Cass smiled. Maybe he'd calmed down, reviewed the plays, and decided he wouldn't keep her on the bench as he had threatened. Things were definitely looking up, she thought.

After the critique, they did some warm-ups and practiced a few plays they were going to initiate on Friday night. Then the coach told them to do two laps and hit the showers.

As they finished the second lap and headed for the door, Turner had a word of encouragement for each of the players. However, when Cass ran past, he said, "See me in my office after you shower, Carothers."

"Sure," Cass answered cheerfully, but she didn't like the look of triumph on his face. It wasn't the same look she had seen after they won the game Tuesday night. It caught her off guard after his friendly manner during practice.

Cass showered for the second time that day, dressed quickly, and ran to the coach's office before any of the rest of the team emerged from the locker room.

"Carothers," the coach said when she walked in the door for the second day in a row, "I've been doing some thinking since we talked yesterday. I've been thinking that basketball is an all-American sport. It was developed in the good old U.S. of A. It's played here more than any other country, and more than any other sport it represents what we are and who we are. It takes intelligence to play basketball. It takes grace, speed, stamina, and guts. When we're out there on the court, we not only show those people in the bleachers who we are as individuals, but we show them how a group of separate people can come together and form a unified team. And it's that team which symbolizes the spirit of our country, Carothers."

"I agree with you, Coach," Cass said, knowing this was building up to something, but unable to understand just what.

"I'm sure you agree that since this game represents America, it should be played by people who also represent America and who don't put Mexicans first."

"But Coach Turner," Cass protested, suddenly getting his drift. "I don't put Mexico or Mexicans first. I put people first. Miguel's my friend."

"Miguel's a Mexican. I'm an American, and I am also your coach. You owe me respect, Carothers. If you don't have enough respect for me to do what I say no matter what, you don't have enough respect for me to play on the team. I can't stop and explain why I'm telling you to make this play or that play. You gotta get out there and do what I say 'cause you believe in me."

"I do believe in you," Cass said. "You're a great coach."

"Then why'd you try to set me up?" the coach asked, picking up a sheet of paper from his desk. Cass reached out for it.

"A xerox copy," he said. "The cops have the original."

"The cops?" Cass asked, scared.

"You didn't think I'd let a thing like this pass by me, did you?" Coach Turner asked.

Cass swallowed and looked down. She read the note, a more coherent version of the one Julio had pieced together.

"I didn't write that," she said softly.

"Oh, I know that, Carothers. Look at the grammar. I'm not that stupid, you know. Miguel Chavez obviously wrote the note, and he obviously wanted to meet me in the parking lot to defend your honor."

"But I didn't know he wrote it," Cass protested.

"You know what? I don't think I believe you. Oh, I can understand Julio's sticking up for his cousin. After all, they're both Mexicans, but you—uh ah. Something's very strange about that. Anybody'd do that would do anything. Ya know, we never had any problems on the team till you came along. Martinez is a good Mexican. I let him play with us 'cause he's as fast as a lightning bolt and he knows his place. He knows when to keep quiet! But you, you come along and get things all stirred up."

"I'm sorry," Cass said. "I didn't mean for this to happen, and I didn't know about the note. Please, believe me," she said as she walked toward the door without waiting for the coach to say anything else.

"Like I said yesterday, Carothers, I'm not gonna stop you from sitting on the bench, but now that you've shown your real colors, I'll never let you near that court."

Cass walked slowly to her car. She knew she wouldn't find Miguel waiting for her today, but she looked around, anyway. No Miguel. No Jackson. No Stevens. No Weiner. No Julio. Everyone had gone home for a pleasant dinner.

CHAPTER SEVENTEEN

"Hey, isn't this the final game of the play-offs?" the Saint called out to her as she was ready to leave the house.

"Yeah," Cass answered quickly, without looking back at him. She put her hand on the doorknob and started to turn it.

"Don't you want us to come?" Saint asked, walking toward her. He put his arm around her shoulder, but she stiffened up instead of relaxing against him, as she usually did.

"That's all right," Cass said. "Tonight's round won't be all that exciting. You can come to the championship game on Saturday."

"What if the Wildcats don't make it to the championship game? We haven't seen you play this season," Saint said. "I feel guilty."

"Well, don't," Cass answered, pulling away from him and walking toward the door. She was in a bad mood, but it wasn't the Saint's fault. She opened the door and called back to him. "We'll win, tonight. Don't worry."

She got into her car and guided it down the hill. Sure, they'd win tonight. It was a cinch, but she wouldn't be responsible for it in any way. Turner had kept his word. Though she had thrown some amazing baskets during warm-ups and had never been in better shape, he hadn't played her once during the last game on Friday night. She had sat smoldering on the bench while he gave every other player a chance on the floor. A few of the guys had mentioned it afterward, but they were all so high from their own performances, they didn't spend much time wondering why she had sat out the game. She thought she had heard the coach saying something to Jackson about its being "that time of the month," but she couldn't believe that Coach Turner would say such a stupid thing. Whatever it was he had said, however, had satisfied anyone interested in why she hadn't played. She wondered what his tactic would be tonight. She wondered what all the people sitting in the bleachers thought about her not playing, or if they even cared. Did they think the coach didn't call her in as a substitute because she wasn't even good enough for that? Maybe she should just turn around right now and not bother going to the game at all. What was the use of suiting up and going through all the warm-ups for nothing? She stopped the car and was about to turn around when she realized that was exactly what the coach expected her to do, give up. It would make his life easier because he wouldn't have to explain anything to anybody. It would also make her life easier—for the moment—but she had never given up on anything before, and now wasn't the time to start a new pattern. She had to go, and she had to find some way of getting into the big game, even if she was forced to sit out tonight's. The scouts would be there on Saturday, damn it, and so would she. She turned the car key again. Willie Boy groaned. He thought he was going to get a chance to rest, and now Cass was grinding him up again. He was obviously not too happy about that. He groaned once again. "Oh, no," Cass yelled, panicking. "If I'm late, he'll really have an excuse not to let me play. Last week, he warned me that that would end my basketball career.

I can't believe this is happening to me," she cried, flooding the gas. This time, Willie Boy didn't even groan. "Okay. Okay, don't panic," Cass said in a panic. "Just relax, breathe deeply. One, two, three, four, five," she counted. She took deep breaths and counted to ten, then she turned the key again. This time the car turned over. "Good boy," she sang and thrust the car into drive. Good thing the game was at school tonight. By now she'd have missed the team bus for Lynwood.

She pulled into the parking lot and looked around. She recognized Weiner's car and Steven's, and the coach's, but none of the rest of the guys were there, yet. Thank goodness, she thought, as she grabbed her stuff and ran to the locker room.

When she had suited up, she walked onto the floor, hoping that someone would toss her a ball so she would feel more comfortable. She suddenly felt awkward. She felt like she was all arms and she didn't know what to do with them. Not only that, her legs felt six feet long, and though she knew they were muscular, she felt as if she were perched on two skinny stilts. Everyone thinks I'm a freak, she thought for the first time in her life. Suddenly, being so tall didn't seem like such an asset, anymore. Everyone's laughing at me she decided, and bent her head to the ground. "Eyes up," Julio cried, and she looked at him in time to see the ball speeding toward her. She caught it, dribbled it a few times, and paused. She stood in front of the basket, holding the ball. "Holding," someone shouted. She wanted to shoot. She wanted desperately to make a basket, but she was afraid to try. What if she didn't make it? Then everyone would know why the coach wasn't using her. They'd think she was really a lousy shooter. "Go for it," Jackson yelled. Instead of shooting, however, she threw the ball to Jackson and walked off the court. Jackson shot, and Julio caught the ball on the rebound. He dribbled it a few times, running close to Cass. He didn't have to say anything. He just shook his head, no. Cass knew what that meant. She could see the sadness in his eyes. Julio paused and rimmed the basket. This time, Weiner caught the ball on the rebound and said jokingly to Julio, "Let's put some muscle into it, babe. You saving yourself for the big game or something?"

"Get off my back, *babe*," Julio sneered.

"Well, *sooooorrrry*," Weiner answered, dribbling away from Julio with a disgusted look.

Turner blew his whistle and called for mirrors. The guys paired off in two's and mirrored each other's moves to practice guarding. Cass's rhythm was off. She couldn't follow Anderson's moves, and she knew that if they had been in an actual game, she could never have grabbed the ball from the guy she was guarding, nor could she have stopped him from making a basket. Her arms fell to her sides like lead. She just couldn't concentrate with Julio moving beside her mirroring Weiner. He was having a hard time of it, too. When Weiner moved his arms up to fake a throw, Julio barely got his raised shoulder-high. "Martinez, wake up, will ya?" Weiner whispered. "We got a game in twenty minutes."

"Go to hell," Julio answered.

"Screw you, Martinez," Weiner shot back angrily.

"You're off tonight, aren't you?" Anderson asked as he continued moving his arms.

"Yeah," Cass answered.

"Come on, Coach is watching," Anderson whispered, encouraging her to move with him, slowing down his movements so that she could keep up.

Cass appreciated Anderson's concern, and she wanted to stop and explain to Weiner and Jackson why Julio was in such a bad mood. She knew it was because he was worried about Miguel, but she also knew that if Julio wanted anyone else to know about Miguel, he himself would tell them. She wanted nothing more than to comfort Julio, to help him and forget her own problems, right now, but she also knew that was impossible. If she tried in any way to come to his defense, it would be the end of whatever relationship they had begun to form the other night. Their friendship was still too new and vulnerable for her to tamper with, and she couldn't afford to do anything to jeopardize that one moment of closeness they had shared.

Warm-ups were winding down, and it was almost time for the first-quarter buzzer. As the team approached the coach for final instructions, Stevens tried to joke with Julio. "Hey, Martinez," he said. "See that guy over there? Number twenty-one?" he asked, pointing to Vince Engle, the best shooter on the Woodland Hills team, who also happened to be six feet seven inches, towering over even Jackson, who was the tallest man on their team at six feet four.

"Yeah? So what?" Julio asked.

"Coach said you were assigned to guard him," Stevens said, suppressing a laugh.

"Shut up, Stevens," Julio snapped.

Cass cringed.

"Come on, Julio," Stevens said laughing. "I was only joking around. Lighten up, will ya?"

"Yeah, what's eatin' you, Martinez?" Jackson asked, joining the conversation. "He was just kidding."

"Nothin'," Julio said. "We're here to play basketball, not to tell jokes."

"Oh, hell, man," Jackson said lightly. "Everybody has a bad day, now and then. Hang in there. The cloud will lift."

Cass held her breath. She didn't know how Julio would take Jackson's comment. She wished she didn't feel so responsible for him, as if his reaction reflected on her in some way.

Julio didn't answer. Cass was relieved. He simply turned his back on Jackson and Weiner and faced the coach. Cass stood next to him, listening to the coach's last-minute advice and good wishes, but she knew they weren't for her. She slid onto the bench while Jackson, Weiner, Julio, Stevens, and Anderson trotted onto the court.

By the fourth quarter, Cass knew that Coach Turner wasn't planning on letting her play basketball tonight, either, and in a way, she was relieved. The self-confidence she had brought to practice that first day, which she had been able to summon up from her slightly humbled unconscious, in spite of the resistance from the rest of the team, in spite of the coach's reluctance to her being there, had suddenly turned to self-doubt. She knew that, sitting somewhere in the bleachers, Coach Morris was wondering why she wasn't playing, but she also knew that even a shout of encouragement for her, at this moment, wouldn't make her feel any better about herself or about her ability to get out there and really do the kind of job that was necessary on a winning team. And if she didn't believe in herself, she could hardly blame the coach for not believing in her. She felt sorry for herself, and she was also sorry that she had changed her mind and come to the game. She realized now that no one would have missed her had she decided to turn around, go home, and crawl into bed, hiding her head under her pillow, along with all her dreams for a scholarship.

Coach Reynolds from the opposing team was signaling a time out. One of his players had twisted his ankle when he jumped for a sky hook. Cass almost smiled as she saw Vince Engle, the giant of the Lynwood team, limp haltingly from the floor. That meant

the game was in the Wildcats' pocket for sure. Coach
Turner relaxed and put in two second stringers who
would probably be part of his starting team next year.
They were only sophomores, but they were tall, and
they were fast. Cass envied them. She began to wish
the coach would call her in, too. But she remembered,
and she sat hunched over on the bench.

The Wildcats won, as predicted, and the crowd went
wild. Even though Lynwood had boasted they had the
most talented big man in the league, they hadn't been
able to pull off a victory. This meant that the Wildcats
would play at the Long Beach Arena on Saturday for
the League Championship, and it also meant that once
again, Cass would be confined to the bench, if she
decided to come to the game at all.

After the shouting died down, both teams returned
to the locker room to change, and the crowd filed out,
congratulating everybody in sight. Cass sat in the gym
alone. Then she quietly got up from the bench and
stared at the baskets, first one, then the other. She
walked onto the court and picked up a ball that had
been left behind in the excitement of victory. She held
it in her hands for several minutes, as if she were
testing it out for the first time, as if she had never seen
a basketball before. Then she dribbled it slowly to the
nearest net and threw it into the hoop. She caught the
ball on the rebound and made another basket and another
one. She wished the crowd could see her, now. She
wished the coach could see her. She wished her team
could see her. Most of all, she wished Julio could see
her.

She stood back at the foul line and shot the ball
again. It whizzed through the air and fell into the hoop.
She *could* play basketball, she thought. She could do
it. At least, she could do it when she was by herself.
Could she do it against another player? Against another

team? And could she actually ever regain that confidence which the coach had managed to squeeze out of her, drop by drop?

She picked up the ball and stood farther back. She took her time, found her rhythm, then calmly shot the free throw and watched it move through the hoop.

She turned suddenly at the bang coming from the doorway. Jackson was standing there, clapping. She blushed, not because she had been caught out there, shooting baskets all by herself, but because she was so glad someone had caught her.

"Nice shot," Jackson said, walking onto the court.

"How come you're not changing?" Cass asked, dribbling the ball.

"I got to thinking that you weren't in the game again tonight, and I got to wondering why," Jackson said. I knocked on the girls' locker-room door, but no one answered, and I didn't hear the shower running, so I thought I'd check to see if you were still out here."

"I'm still out here," she said, trying to tuck the ball under her arm. It slipped out and hit the floor. They both laughed, breaking the tension. Jackson picked up the ball and said, "Let's practice a little defense. We know you can score."

For the next forty-five minutes, until the plant supervisor came to turn off the lights, Fred Jackson and Cass played one on one, and in spite of the fact that Jackson had just played a full game, he gave this his best shot, too. Cass, who had sat out the game, was wild with unreleased energy, and Jackson couldn't keep her down. She made basket after basket, and she hounded him time and time again, preventing him from scoring. Her defense was tenacious. She was unbeatable, though she was a bit off when it came to her long-range jumper. Jackson gave her some pointers, and she tried again and again until she could make those baskets almost as easily as she could make a basket on a free throw, which was her speciality.

When they finally had to leave the gym, Jackson told her to hurry up and change so they could meet all the guys at the Santa Monica Cafe.

"You sure?" she asked. "Am I invited?"

"Hell, yeah," Jackson shouted. "You're on the team, aren't you?"

"I guess so," Cass answered, suddenly realizing that Jackson hadn't really asked her why she had sat out the game. "But I'm not sure the coach knows."

"Forget him," Jackson said. "At least for tonight. Come on. Get your stuff."

"Thanks, Fred," Cass said, looking at him, filled to the eyeballs with gratitude.

"Shit," Jackson said, turning into the locker room. "Don't thank me. I need a ride over there, and you're the only one still around with a car."

CHAPTER EIGHTEEN

Cass squeezed into a parking space on Twenty-first Street, and she and Jackson entered the brightly lit Santa Monica Cafe, one of the few places in town open all night. Though they had recently remodeled to improve their image, hoping to attract the more affluent folks in the area, the cafe still served as a hangout for high-school and college kids and the various arty types—writers and actors who lived nearby. At just about any time of day or night, you could walk in and see at least three people writing or studying scripts. There was always one large round table filled with students. The big table in the back was now jammed with various members of the basketball team, and several smaller tables nearby caught the overflow. Everyone was already eating by the time Jackson and Cass walked in. Cass noticed that there was room for one person to squeeze in at the big table, next to Julio, and there was room for one person at a smaller table. She didn't want to appear too anxious, so she urged Jackson to sit down at the big table, but he had already begun talking to Stevens, who was sitting in a booth. As if it were an afterthought, Cass slipped in next to Julio and ordered fried zucchini, the house specialty.

Spirits at the table were high, and everybody seemed to have forgotten Julio's moodiness earlier in the evening, including Julio. Cass noticed, however, that he was very quiet, barely saying a word while the other

guys placed bets on the spread of the championship
game. Sure they were going to cream Glendale, Weiner
bet they'd win by twenty points.

"You know something we don't, Weiner?" Raden
asked.

"What do you mean?" Weiner answered. "I got confidence in you guys, that's all."

"Hey, confidence is great," Raden said, "But over-
confidence means you're either an egomaniac, or you
heard somebody's gotten to Glendale. I mean, we're
good, man, but we're not that good. We're not good
enough to beat them by twenty points. I'd say we could
maybe go ten at the most, unless they're planning to
throw the game."

"Well, I'd say fifteen," Joey Rubin interjected, "even
if they are planning to throw it."

Everyone laughed except Anderson. "Hey, man,
that's no joke," he said. "There was a case like that a
coupla years ago. Some Mafia-type guy paid off a
player to throw a game."

"A college player," Raden said.

"No," Anderson corrected him, "some high-school
player in a championship game."

"A high-school player?" Rubin asked, amazed.
"What kind of a kid would screw his team like that?"

"How much did he get?" Raden asked.

"A bundle," Anderson answered. "Ten, twelve
thousand bucks."

"You kidding, man? What's his number?" Rubin
asked, taking a pencil out of his pocket. "I gotta save
up some dough for college, or better yet, buy me a
little sailboat," he said, laughing.

"I heard there're going to be some scouts from the
east there Saturday night," Anderson said. "Makes me
nervous as hell."

"Me, too," Raden agreed. "I wish they wouldn't

tell us about that stuff. It's hard enough to concentrate on the game without having to remember you're being scouted like a bunch of cattle."

"Horses," Rubin corrected. "I hear that after the game they check out your teeth and the bottom of your feet, so they can tell if you're healthy."

"I wouldn't be surprised," Weiner said. "I'm just glad I don't have to depend on them for a college education. I think my grades are good enough to get into Berkeley, and that's where I want to go. My grandparents put away some money for me, and my parents can help; with my summer job, I'll be able to make it without basketball."

"Aren't you going to play at Berkeley?" Rubin asked, amazed.

"I don't think so," Weiner mused. "Even though it'll be hard to resist playing in the Pac Ten."

"I don't understand," Raden said. "Why would you want to go to college if you couldn't play ball?"

"Believe it or not, Raden, there are other reasons for going to college," Weiner said, patronizing Tony.

"Yeah, I guess so," Tony said. Then he looked at Weiner with a straight face. "What other reasons?"

This really cracked everybody up, including Julio, who hadn't said one word during the whole conversation till now. "Raden," he said, "you're one of a kind."

"Wrong," Raden said, laughing. "I have a twin brother."

"Raden, don't give us that garbage," Anderson said. "You never had any twin brother unless your family drowned him. One of you is all your parents could take."

"Actually, one of me is more than my parents could take," Tony said. "I'm an orphan. Now give me that damn phone number. I'm a poor kid who has to put

himself through college. You guys will understand if
I just shave ten points or so off the game. We can still
win."

"Raden!" Anderson and Rubin said together, menacing him from either side.

"Wait till I tell your mother you're an orphan,"
Weiner said. "She'll probably be relieved as hell."

"Okay, so I'm not an orphan," Tony admitted, "but
if I don't get home pretty soon, my parents will lock
me out of the house, and I will be."

"Yeah, I gotta go, too," Anderson said. "Anybody
need a ride?"

"I'm going with Weiner," Rubin said.

"Cass?" Anderson asked.

"I got my car," she answered. "I can drive anyone,"
she said, hoping Julio would take her up on the offer.
He didn't.

They divvied up the check and everyone got up to
leave after saying good-bye to the guys who were still
shoveling down food. Cass went to the ladies' room
on the way out, and when she came back into the
restaurant, everyone from her table had gone. She
wondered how Julio was getting home.

She walked toward her car and noticed a familiar
figure standing at the bus stop on the corner. She
couldn't see all that well in the dark, but she thought
she recognized Julio by the slant of his shoulders.

"Julio?" she called.

"Yeah," he answered.

"Come on," she said. "I'm going in your direction."

"It's out of the way," he answered.

"I want to talk to you, anyway," she said, "about—
you know." She wanted to give him a reason for coming with her, so they could talk in private.

He ambled over to the car, casually looking around
to see if anyone was watching him. Cass shook her

head in disbelief. Most guys wouldn't mind being seen with her, she thought. Anderson had asked her out a few times, and she knew that Weiner had a crush on her.

They got into the car and drove to the edge of Santa Monica, next to Venice. Julio told her they had had no word from Miguel, and that his family had no idea what had happened to him. He had gotten in touch with his parents, but they hadn't heard from him, either. "I can't imagine anyone hurting that guy," Julio said. "But he's too dumb to protect himself. He thinks he's so tough, but he hates any kind of fight. If someone came up and demanded his money, he'd give him his shirt, too."

"He'll turn up," Cass said, trying to reassure Julio, though she wasn't at all sure she was right.

"Maybe," Julio said, "but in what condition? He can't have more than five, ten bucks on him, and he's already been gone a week. It makes me crazy. I can't think about anything else."

"After the game on Saturday, we'll have more time to look for him," she said.

"Yeah—the game," Julio said. "That game is my ticket out of here, away from these kinds of worries."

"Mine, too," Cass said quietly.

Julio turned to Cass as if seeing her for the first time. "Yours?" he asked.

"Think I've been taking all that abuse for nothing?" she laughed. "I would have stayed on the girls' team and been their star player, but I need a scholarship or I can't go to college, even if I go to UCLA and live at home. We just don't have the bucks. I had to do something to attract attention, but it looks like it was just a waste of time," she added. "I don't think Turner's going to let me play on Saturday night, either."

"If Miguel hadn't already threatened him, I'd do it

myself," Julio laughed. "I know it's not funny, but that guy is screwing more people than Anderson, and Anderson was worried about three different ladies last month."

"Anderson?" Cass laughed and made a mental note to say no the next time he asked her out. She had never heard Julio joke around before. She liked it. This was a different side of him.

"Where do you want to go to school?" she asked.

"UCLA's my first choice. I can play ball and get a decent education. The education's what counts. The game will only buy it for me. I'm nothing without a college degree; but a Chicano with an education— look out!"

"I hope you get it," she said softly. She added to herself, that she hoped he got the scholarship even if she didn't.

Cass pulled up in front of Julio's house. "How many brothers and sisters do you have?" she asked, knowing there were two or three at school besides Julio.

"Only seven," he laughed. "But we got two bedrooms."

"You must sleep on the ceiling."

"It's just you Anglos who need so much space. You don't like each other. We like each other. We like to be close. Even if I have plenty of money some day, I'm still gonna live with my family." He laughed again. "Only maybe I'll buy us a bigger house."

Cass laughed, too. She wanted to lean over and quickly kiss him on the cheek. He was so damn cute. But she didn't want to scare him away. He leaned toward her. She closed her eyes, but he just sort of patted her head, whispered a thank-you, and disappeared before she could open her eyes again. The coach was right about one thing, she thought. Julio did move like lightning.

CHAPTER NINETEEN

"Wanna go for a ride in the hills?" the Saint asked when Cass woke up and ventured out into the kitchen for breakfast.

"Sure," she said, rubbing her eyes.

"Get dressed. I want to get in some time before it starts to rain," her father said, looking out of the window.

"It isn't going to rain," Cass said, scavenging through the cupboard for some cereal.

"Yes, it is. I can always tell by the feel of the wood."

"That's a new one," Cass said, pouring some granola and milk into a bowl. "Most people can tell if it's going to rain because their bones ache."

"I'm too young to have aching bones," Saint laughed. "How fast can you get ready?"

"Oh, go on without me," she said, pushing the spoon around in her bowl.

"Don't feel well, or got pre-game jitters?" Saint asked, looking at her.

"Neither," she answered. "I just changed my mind, is all."

"Okay," he said, giving her a squeeze.

He walked out of the kitchen and called to Sky, who was working in the garden. "Wanna go for a ride?"

"No," she yelled back. "I want to finish this before it rains."

"Well, I'm going anyway," he said. "The horses haven't been ridden all week."

"Be back in time for lunch?" Sky asked.

Cass didn't hear his answer as he disappeared into the barn. A few minutes later, she heard him ride off. She was about to call him and tell him she had changed her mind and wanted to ride, after all, but then she decided not to keep him waiting. She wasn't dressed yet, anyway.

Sky came in, carrying a basketful of winter vegetables, which she set down on the counter.

"Hi, babe," she said. "You slept later than usual, today."

"I was tired," Cass said, yawning. "In fact, I think I'll go lie down again after breakfast."

"You okay?" Sky asked, feeling Cass's forehead.

"Yeah," Cass sighed. "I guess so."

"Well, you don't have a temperature, but you could be coming down with the flu or something. Let me make you some herb tea."

"Forget it," Cass said. "Herb tea doesn't cure anything. It just makes me want to puke."

"Boy, you're in a good mood," Sky said. "Pre-game jitters?"

"Why does everybody think I have pre-game jitters?" Cass said irritably. "I'm just in a bad mood, is all."

She shoved her bowl across the table. The milk spilled out and dripped onto the floor, but she just sat there watching it flow off the varnished wood. She could have stopped it, but she didn't feel like it.

"You spilled your milk," Sky said, turning around.

"No kidding?" Cass said sarcastically, as she got up and grabbed some paper towels. The minute she opened her mouth she was sorry she had been so bitchy, but

she didn't feel much like apologizing, so she just
mopped up the milk and kept her back to Sky.

"Okay, let's have it," Sky demanded. "You haven't
been so obnoxious since you were four years old.
Remember when I made you wear that furry white
sweater, and you insisted it was too ugly and it itched?
You said you were embarrassed, and you wouldn't be
caught dead in it, and I told you, you would be caught
dead pretty soon if you didn't march into your room
and get it, 'cause it was very chilly out. You ran off,
kicking the furniture on the way, singing under your
breath, just loud enough for me to hear you, 'Sky
i-i-is stupid. *Stupi-i-i-d Sky-y-y.*'"

Cass started to laugh. "Well, it was ugly," she said.
"It probably ruined my whole childhood by making
me an outcast. No wonder I'm in a bad mood," she
said, pretending to be serious. "It's all your fault. If
you hadn't made me wear that stupid sweater, I'd be
on the girls' team, like any other sane female; I wouldn't
be on the boys' team making an ass out of myself."

"Oh—" Sky said, her ears suddenly picking up a
signal from Cass, a signal which had been carefully
coded before.

"Oh, nothing," Cass said. "I was just kidding. Put
your *Psychology for Everyday Living* back on the shelf.
I'm just in a bad mood."

"You must be, since you didn't eat your breakfast,"
Sky said, eyeing the granola left in the bowl. "I know
what, let's go over to the Inn for lunch."

"Okay," Cass said with less than her usual enthusiasm. Then she shrugged her shoulders. "No, I don't
want to eat anything heavy before the game. Besides,
I think you're right. I might be coming down with
something, and maybe you shouldn't plan on coming
all the way to Long Beach, anyway, 'cause I might
not feel well enough to play, I mean, I might feel well

enough to go, I'm not sure, but I might have to ask the coach not to put me in the game, and then you'll be upset 'cause you won't know what's going on, and you'll have to sit there the whole time and not even see me play, and how will you get there, anyway?" she said in one breath.

"Oh," Sky said, "I see."

"It's not what you think," Cass said. "I just don't want you to bother coming, is all."

"But we want to," Sky insisted.

"Well, this is a stupid discussion 'cause I don't think I'll even go."

"I see," Sky said again, turning back to the sink, but not before Cass noticed the worried look on her face. She wanted to tell Sky what was wrong. She knew her mother would not only understand, she would be delighted that her daughter had finally become a political activist. And that wasn't what she wanted to talk about right now. That wasn't why she had defended Miguel. She had defended him because he was her friend. His being Mexican had nothing to do with it. That was just a coincidence. If she told her mother about it, her mother would just go on and on about how they had protested at Berkeley during the free speech movement, and she didn't think she could stand another Mario Savio story. The real reason she didn't want to confide in her mother, however, had nothing to do with the free speech movement or any other movement. It had to do with the fact that in their family, they had reversed roles. She had taken on the role of mother, and Sky had taken on the role of daughter, and Cass felt she had to protect her mother, just as she had been doing for the past four or five years.

Cass got up from the table feeling ancient. She started to drag herself out of the kitchen, but her mother came up behind her and put her arms around her. No wonder she felt like the adult in the relationship. Here was this tiny woman, barely over five feet high, trying to console a girl of six feet, who could blow her away with a flick of her hand.

Cass started to laugh. "You're such a shrimp," she said.

"Yeah, well, this shrimp is your mother," Sky said. "You sure you don't want to tell me anything?" She gave Cass a gentle hug. Cass turned around. "I'm here if you need me," Sky added. "In fact, I'm here for you whether you need me or not."

Cass almost started to cry. What is this? she asked herself. One minute I'm mad, the next minute I'm laughing, and the next minute I feel like crying. She rested her head on Sky's shoulder like she used to when she was a little girl. "Thanks, Mom," she said.

She wanted to go on. She wanted to tell her mother about the way she was being treated by the coach, but she was somehow embarrassed. Not that it was really her fault, or anything, but she somehow felt guilty, maybe for jeopardizing her scholarship, knowing what their financial circumstances were. She knew it was irrational, but hell, even she couldn't be rational all the time. "Mom," she began, then burst into tears while still deciding whether or not to confide in her mother.

"Everyone needs to do that once in a while," Sky said, while Cass was wiping her tears on the sleeve of her terry-cloth bathrobe.

"At least this robe absorbs water," Cass said, laughing and crying at the same time.

"Okay, now don't forget what I told you to say," Sky said seriously. "Tell Coach Turner if he doesn't put you in the game tonight, I'm going to be there with my hammer and nails, and if he values his knee caps—"

"What kind of talk is that from a nonviolent person?" Cass said, still sniffling a little.

"Well, everybody has at least one thing they're willing to go to the mats for," Sky said, "and what's a better cause than your kid?"

Luckily, the phone rang before Cass started to cry again, and she ran to answer it.

"Okay, Carothers," Kathy said on the other end of the line, "the entire girls' basketball team and Coach Morris are going to be there rooting for you, tonight. Now, do us proud, girl."

"I might not go," Cass said quietly, so her mother wouldn't hear.

"What?" Kathy screamed into the mouthpiece. "You're not gonna let that stupid turkey get to you. You! The kid with all the guts. Come on, you have to go. You never give up, Cass. Now get yourself psyched for that game. I know you're going to play, and I know you're going to be terrific."

"I see you've consulted the oracle at Delphi," Cass said sarcastically.

"No," Kathy said. "Better than that. I called Coach Morris and told her what Turner was pulling on you."

"Kathy, I told you not to tell anybody," Cass said, then quickly added, "What'd she say?"

"She didn't say anything for a long time, then she just said, 'Okay, McCleary, thanks for calling.'"

"So what does that prove?" Cass asked.

"She called Turner right away."

"Another sign from the oracle?"

"Not exactly. I waited for a few minutes and dialed her number again. It was busy. Then I dialed Turner's number. It was busy, too."

"You're wild, McCleary," Cass said laughing. "I'm going to kill you for doing this to me. After the game, of course."

"Of course," Kathy said. "See you later."

"I'm starving," Cass yelled when she got off the phone. She ran into the kitchen and made herself some eggs, toast, juice, and sliced tomatoes, humming all the while.

CHAPTER TWENTY

When the Saint returned from his ride, his clothes were slightly damp. "It's drizzling," he said. "I got back just in time." He shivered. "Winter's really here, ladies," he added as he went to shower and change.

Cass threw a few logs into the fireplace and sat down to do some homework. She opened her social studies book and began reading, but after a half hour, the words started jumping around and the heat from the fireplace made her drowsy. The sound of the wood crackling and sputtering finally lulled her to sleep.

Even before she opened her eyes, she heard a steady pinging sound on the roof. It was pleasant, not a heavy beat but a light tapping, as if elves were dancing around in the puddles on top of the house. She smiled and snuggled into the warm, comfortable pillows before she opened her eyes and looked at her watch. It was almost three o'clock. She had to be out of the house by five-thirty to make the bus, which would leave school for Long Beach at six.

She decided to do a few loosening-up exercises, just to get the kinks out. She had been lazing around all day and felt pretty stiff. When she finished, she ambled into the kitchen and grabbed an apple, thinking she'd have something more substantial right before she left the house, to give her energy for the game.

She looked out of the kitchen window and watched the rain as it fell steadily, the pinging becoming more like a pounding, now. It was still early, but dark clouds covered the sky, shutting out any remnants of daylight, and Cass had to turn on the kitchen lights.

"It's really coming down," Sky said, standing in the doorway. "It'll be good for my garden if it doesn't get any harder. If it gets worse, though, we're going to have trouble."

"I hope not," Cass said absentmindedly. For some reason, what her mother had just said made her slightly uncomfortable for a moment, but she couldn't figure out why, so she dismissed whatever it was and decided to make a few phone calls just to pass the time. She was too nervous to do any more homework. As she walked toward her room, she called back to her mother, "You and Saint can come if you want to, but you don't have to."

"Well, thanks," her mother said. "Never thought you'd ask. We'll drive you to school, drop you off and head for Long Beach."

"You sure you remember how to drive?" Cass called back.

"It's like riding a bike," Sky answered. "Once you learn—wait a minute," she hesitated. "Is that really true? I don't think I can remember how to shift gears."

"In a car or on a bike?" Cass asked, laughing.

"Get out of here before you drive me bananas," Sky laughed. "I'm going to fix you something with lots of protein, so you'll have enough energy for two people."

"One will do," Cass said, as she walked into her room.

She picked up the phone and tried to decide whom to call.

She had already spoken to Kathy for half an hour. There wasn't much more she could say to her. She could call Lisa or Carrie, but she hadn't really talked to either of them since basketball season started. She'd been so busy that she had lost touch with all her old friends, except Kathy. Still thinking, she held the phone in her hand. When it rang, she fell off the bed and dropped the phone as if it were on fire. Instead of picking it up, she stared at it for a moment.

"Can you get that?" Sky called from the kitchen.

Cass breathed deeply and picked up the phone. "Hello," she said, her voice shaking slightly.

"Listen, about those shots from the foul line. Remember to keep your arms raised as high above your shoulders as you can, and keep your eye on the front of the rim, no matter what."

"Jackson?"

"You been practicing one on one with anyone else?" Jackson laughed.

"Thanks, Jackson."

"Okay. So, see you over at school pretty soon, right?"

"Yeah," Cass said, grinning.

She hung up the phone and hugged herself. Then she fooled around in her room, straightening things up, not too much, of course; then she wouldn't be able to find anything. By the time she checked her watch, again, it was almost five. She dashed into the bathroom for a shower and let the hot water pour over her as she sang.

When she stepped out of the shower, she thought she had forgotten to turn off the faucets, before she realized that the sound of pounding water was coming from outside. She couldn't see out of the opaque window, but it sure seemed as if the rain had begun to come down even harder.

By the time she was dressed and in the kitchen for dinner, it was pitch black outside, and the rain had turned into a storm, moving the trees around so brutally that they punished the roof and sides of the house in retaliation. It was beginning to make her nervous, and her mother's pacing around the kitchen, worrying about her garden, didn't help much, either. Saint was in the barn trying desperately to patch up a hole in the ceiling from the inside, so the horses would stay dry. But Sky said that each time he fixed one hole, water started pouring in from someplace else. This was the worst storm they'd seen in years. Cass was glad when it was time to go; she would, at least, have something to do besides worry about the weather.

"Listen, sweet pea," Saint said, walking into the house, his slicker dripping. "I'm just not going to be able to make it to the game. I have to patch up three or four more places, or everything will be ruined, I'm afraid, including the winter's supply of hay."

"That's okay," Cass said, though she was disappointed.

"Look," Sky said. "I just can't stand here and see my beautiful garden ruined. She began running around the kitchen gathering up large plastic bags. "I'm going out there to cover it up. I'm sorry, honey."

"I understand," Cass said. She kissed both of them, grabbed her keys, put on her heavy raincoat, and ran out to her car as they wished her luck.

Willie Boy turned over right away, as if the rain had washed him off and given him new life. "Good for you, Boy," she said. "I was almost afraid you were going to give me trouble. She let the car warm up for a few minutes, then she put it in reverse and tried to back it out of the driveway. The tire spun around, splashing mud in every direction. She stopped and rocked the car back and forth, trying to ease it out, but it didn't work. She stopped, and once again tried to thrust it into reverse and out of the driveway.

The car stalled. She panicked and pumped the gas. It started again, but she couldn't get it to move. She broke into a sweat. She was going to be late. She would miss the bus. She would miss her chance to play in the championship game.

Determined, she rocked the car again, but instead of lifting the car out of its cradle, she pushed it farther into the mud, which was, by now, up to the top of her fenders.

She swung open the car door, leaped out, and ran into the kitchen. "Mom, help me. The car's stuck," she cried.

Sky pulled on her raincoat and dropped the pile of plastic bags. First, she ran to get Saint from the barn, then they joined Cass at the car. Cass got inside and put the car into neutral as her mother and father pushed. It moved. It swayed. It was almost out. She was about to start the engine and put it into reverse, when the car dropped back into the hole.

"It's no use," Saint said. "I'll go next door to see if we can use the Franks' car."

"I'll try the Simmons," Sky said, running in the other direction.

Cass looked at her watch and called them back. It was too late. Even if they could find an available car, she would never get to school in time to hop the bus to Long Beach.

Sky put her arm around Cass. "Sorry, honey. Come on in. I'll make some hot tea."

"Go on," Cass said. "I'm going to try one more time."

Her mother walked back to the house to gather her plastic bags, and her father went back to his work in the barn. Cass tried the car again, knowing it was futile. She pumped and pushed and it didn't move an inch. She put her head down on the steering wheel and cried.

Suddenly, there was a blinding light aimed at her. She raised her head and looked up into it, then shielded her eyes. She couldn't see who it was, but someone was standing next to the car holding a huge flashlight pointed directly at her. She could also hear the sound of a running engine. She tried to look around the light.

"Hurry up," Julio called.

"Julio!" she said, leaping out of the car.

He opened the door of the jeep for her and told her to get in quickly.

"But—but," she sputtered.

"Come on."

She scrambled onto the high seat, and they took off with ease down the muddy driveway, onto the debris-laden street, and headed toward Pacific Coast Highway, which had not yet been closed off, but, by the look of things, would be by morning.

"Where did you get this?" Cass asked. "What are you doing here, and how did you know I was stuck?"

"I borrowed the jeep," Julio said, watching the road very carefully. "I came to get you because I realized you must be stuck. I remembered this muddy road and your driveway, and when everyone else showed up at school but you, well, I figured there was no way Willie Boy was going to make it."

"But, but—the game. The bus. It must have left by now."

"Yeah," Julio said casually.

"We'll never make it."

"We'll make it. We're heading straight for Long Beach. They don't have that much of a head start."

Cass prayed to all the gods she could think of and silently wished she believed in them, now that it really counted. She sat very still, watching the road ahead, as if she were driving, too. Julio seemed very engrossed in his task, anyway, and didn't seem to want to talk. She tried to bite a few of her nails, but they were already bitten down, so she bit her bottom lip, instead, and checked her watch every two or three minutes.

When they pulled into the parking lot of the Long Beach Arena, it was completely dark. At first they thought they must have come to the wrong place, but they got out to see where they were, anyway. As they approached the huge building, all the lights came on and they realized that the electricity must have gone off because of the storm.

Without saying a word to each other, they ran into the locker rooms to change. When Cass entered the girls' locker room, she could hear Julio being greeted in the locker room next door. The team had been in the middle of changing when the lights went out. They were still getting ready. She was safe.

CHAPTER TWENTY-ONE

Cass ran out onto the floor with the Wildcats and the Roadrunners from Glendale. She was in top form, ready to go, ready to take the ball, make a nice soft throw, and lay it in the basket. Both teams were sizing each other up, trying to psych each other out, glom onto any weakness on either side. The tension was high, but they were all trying to check it until the game actually began.

By the time the referee blew his whistle and the ten starters had gathered in the center for the toss-up, the crowd had become just as tense as the teams. Cass knew that this game meant almost as much to the spectators as it did to the kids who were playing. She looked up into the bleachers and tried to get a glimpse of Kathy or Coach Morris, but the crowd was so large, she couldn't find them. She did spot several of the kids from her English class, however, and some of the other teachers.

She sat on the bench and watched each move, carefully studying what was happening, waiting for her chance to go in and replace Stevens or Julio. Not that she particularly wanted to replace either one of them, but she knew that if she were going to play, that's the way it would happen. Essentially, she and Julio could do the same things well. They were the fastest members of the team and could carry the ball down the court in less time than any of the other guys. In a pinch, when time was running short, they depended on her or Julio to get them to the basket in time. And she and Stevens were both good at free throws. She wished she had been able to start with the Wildcats, but she knew that even if she were the best, the coach wouldn't let her do that. Jackson, Weiner, Stevens, Julio, and Anderson had played on the team for three years. She couldn't expect Turner to dump one of them for her, and she wouldn't want him to. What she wanted was just a chance to get out there for a few minutes during the game and do her stuff and show those scouts hidden out there someplace what kind of a player she was.

The first quarter went well for the Wildcats, though the game was, by no means, in their pocket. They had a slight edge over Glendale, but Glendale's defense was superb, and the size of their players was nothing short of miraculous. Cass realized that when she finally got to the floor, she would be the shortest player, except for Julio, by about three inches.

During the second quarter, with fifty-five seconds to go, Stevens suddenly twisted his ankle as he came down after an off-balance jumper. He made the shot, but he had come down on his foot the wrong way. Signaling a time-out, he motioned to the coach, who helped him hobble off the floor, while the referee made a T, for time, putting the fingers of his left hand into the palm of his right.

Turner called in Raden to replace Stevens, and Raden got up, obviously surprised that he hadn't chosen Cass. Raden, however, was no more surprised than Cass was.

The game got underway again, with a nice pass by Weiner to Julio, who pushed the ball down the court until he was stopped by Funess from Glendale. Funess took the ball, elbowing Weiner out of the way, and the referee called a foul, giving Jackson the ball at the foul line.

As the buzzer sounded, ending the second quarter, there was a steal by Julio, but he couldn't hold onto it, and the score was now Wildcats 59, Roadrunners 60.

It was clear at halftime that Stevens would sit out the rest of the game, and the coach called the team together to revise the strategy for the second half.

The second half began well. Jackson took the ball to the hoop, made a slam dunk, and almost immediately regained the ball and buried another one. The Wildcats were in the lead, and that seemed to be a good sign. Even without Stevens, they were playing excellent ball, Cass thought. She was itching to get in there and play it with them. She fidgeted on the bench, wondering when Turner was going to signal for a time-out and call her in as a substitute, as he had already called in several of the other players to spell Jackson, Julio, Anderson and Weiner.

An attempted bounce pass by Raden to Jackson was intercepted by Glendale, and things began to take a turn for the worse as time was running out in the third quarter. Finally, Julio snared the ball from Glendale, but was called for reaching.

At the end of the third quarter, the score was Wildcats 89, Roadrunners 95. Cass remained on the bench.

The fourth quarter began with a call on Jackson for charging. The boys were getting edgy, Cass thought. They were losing it. She wanted desperately to get in there, just to calm them down, relax them a little, tell them they could do it. Instead, she sat on the bench and watched the coach jump up and down, furious with just about everyone on the team, swearing to himself and clenching his fists.

Cass watched Funess, from Glendale, steal the ball

from Anderson. She jumped up in sympathy, dying to
get out there and grab it back. Funess couldn't hold
the ball. Jackson saved it and made a nice throw to
Julio, who dribbled it down the court, fired it past
Glendale back to Jackson. Jackson jammed it through.
The tide began to turn again, and in the next few
minutes, Anderson caught the ball on a rebound, made
a basket, and then scored on a free throw a few minutes
later. Julio was able to prevent Glendale from making
a basket, stealing the ball from them and taking it to
the hoop for a two pointer himself. Cass stood up and
cheered. She looked at the clock. Only four more
minutes to go. She looked at the coach. Maybe in the
excitement, he had forgotten that she was supposed to
play. She coughed, hoping he'd look up at her, but his
eyes were on the floor. By now, the Wildcats were
leading by five points. Why didn't he send her in?

Suddenly, Cass looked up to see Julio wince in pain.
Turner saw it, too, and called a time-out. Then the
coach and Raden went over to him and helped him off
the floor. He sat down on the bench next to Stevens.
Cass threw him a sympathetic look, but she was afraid
to say anything. She held her breath. She was sorry
Julio had hurt himself. She wouldn't have wanted that
to happen for anything, even if it meant her not getting
into the game, but since it did happen, she was gearing
up, ready to go in there and run the ball down the
court. She was rested and fresh, and she would show
them she was in top form tonight.

Turner indicated to Whitehouse that he would substitute for Julio. Whitehouse got up and ran onto the
court. Cass heard the announcer say, "Arnie Whitehouse, number twenty-five, will substitute for Julio
Martinez, who has been injured."

Jackson called a time-out and ran over to Turner.
Cass was in a daze, shocked at what had just happened.

Julio seemed to be standing up, and Jackson was quietly screaming at Turner, "You got to play Carothers, Coach. We're in there to win this game, not to fight any vendettas. We're never going to see any trophy with Whitehouse in there. Carothers can run faster than anyone on the team, and what we need now is speed. Put her in the game, Coach. Please."

"You're out of line, Jackson," Cass heard Turner answer, but his voice seemed far away, as in a dream.

"So are you," Jackson said. "We got one thing to do—win the game," Jackson spat out. "This is my last game at Samohi, and I don't want to see it go down the tubes. Do you?"

Jackson turned around and sped back to the floor. Turner called to Whitehouse, who returned to the bench, and before she quite realized what was happening, Cass was out on the floor with the Wildcats, playing for the first time in two weeks. She grinned at Jackson, and he grinned back, as the whistle blew, and the referee threw the ball into the air, once more. Both teams were keyed up, now. The game was close, and time was precious. But Cass had something on everyone else. She was electric with unused energy and more than ready to play. There was no keeping her down as she moved up and down the court as if her feet had wings, waving her arms in inspired defensive motions, guarding Lansing from Glendale as he tried to score. She was so wired that she completely threw him off, and the ball fell short of the hoop, allowing Jackson to snare on the rebound. He dribbled the ball down the court and passed to Stevens, who passed to Rubin. Rubin slammed it in. Lansing picked up the ball at the boundary line and tossed it toward Funess, but Cass recovered his errant pass and wove in and out, evading the opposing team until she got to the key, where, to everyone's surprise except Jackson's, she fired in two points. Whistles and cheers went up from the crowd, and Cass flushed with excitement and victory. She was sure she heard Kathy's voice above the crowd, screaming and cheering, and she knew she recognized Coach Morris's whistle of encouragement. This was her moment. She could do anything. And she did. Before the final whistle, she managed another basket on a free throw, and she managed to drive Lansing totally crazy, though he was one of Glendale's best guards. He was completely baffled by her quick movements, aggressive tactics, and unbearable energy.

With the reverberation of the final whistle still ringing in their ears, the crowd leaped to the floor to congratulate their heroes. The Wildcats had taken the trophy, 110–108. Cass was soaked through and through with sweat, and her hair, which had been pulled back and tied securely, was now dripping wet and had come undone. But she was happy. She was very happy. As the team danced to the locker room, everyone was happy. Only Stevens, who cheered with his team, hobbled to the exit. Wait a minute, Cass thought, suddenly. She ran to catch up with Julio, who was at that moment leaping into the air with excitement.

"What happened to your sprained ankle?" she asked as she fell into step with him.

He stopped jumping and limped slightly. "Oh, it was only a momentary sprain," he lied.

"I don't believe it," she said. "You did that for me."

"Nah," Julio answered. "I did it for me. Meet you at the jeep in ten minutes. We have to get back to school before the bus does. Hurry up."

He rushed to the locker room, and Cass walked—actually, she floated—into the girls' locker room. She rushed through her shower, washed her hair quickly, dried it for a few minutes, grabbed her athletic bag and raced to the parking lot, her still damp hair clinging to her. Luckily, however, it had stopped raining. In fact, the sky looked clear, and the air was fresh and clean. After a heavy rain, when everything was hushed and new, clean and crisp, it always felt like the beginning of the world to Cass. She always felt expectant and full of hope. She could, at these times, almost understand why Sky and the Saint spent so much time searching for their truths. She felt both electrified and at peace. She was at one with the world, right now, and there was no one she wanted to share this feeling with more than Julio, who was standing beside the jeep, its engine running, waiting for her.

When they pulled into the school parking lot, Julio took out a piece of paper and a pen. Cass looked over his shoulder as he wrote.

Thanks for your jeep. It was an emergency.
This is for the gas.

He took out some bills from his pocket and attached them to the note.

"What?" Cass screamed. "You stole somebody's car?"

Julio turned the paper over.

You ought to put an alarm on your car.
It's very easy to hot wire.

"You're terrible," Cass yelled, laughing, as they got out of the car.

"I'm worse than that," Julio answered. "I don't even have a license."

"You're insane."

"You're right," Julio said. "But I didn't think Weiner's mother would really throw a fit. After all, what's team spirit about, anyway?"

"You really are crazy," Cass said, looking at Julio.

"Luckily, Weiner couldn't get his car out, either, so his mother let him use her jeep," Julio said. "See, it was meant to be. I just realized that and took advantage of it."

"Thanks," Cass said, putting her hand on his arm. "Thanks for everything."

They stood there for a moment, very close together. Cass could feel her face getting red. She was glad it was dark. She could feel her hands begin to sweat, and she could feel that peculiar throbbing in her neck which beat an announcement to the world every time she got excited about something. Julio leaned toward her as the Samohi bus rolled into the parking lot and pulled up next to them. The team and the coach got out, still singing and laughing, still in a fantastic mood.

Turner came over to Cass and Julio. "You two got away before I had a chance to talk to you," he said uncomfortably. He paused for a long moment. "You both played superior ball," he added. Cass and Julio stood there without responding, as if by mutual agreement they had decided to stand their ground and not give Turner an inch of satisfaction after what he had put them through during basketball season and what he was still putting them through because of Miguel. "Look," he continued. "We're all under a lot of pressure during basketball season. Sometimes we say things we really don't mean." Cass and Julio remained silent. "You know what I mean?" the coach asked.

"No," Julio answered. "I don't know what you mean."

"I'm not saying that I like all the foreigners here," the coach said slowly. "Sometimes I think I'm in the middle of Mexico City when I walk around the school, but I'm sorry I came down on Miguel," Coach Turner admitted. "He's a good kid. He works hard. He's not lazy like the re—like some other kids."

"No, he's not lazy," Julio said, still not giving an inch.

"I just wanted to say that—well—I don't mind if Miguel comes back to class. I noticed he hasn't been in school for the past few weeks. I guess he's afraid to come back, and—"

Cass watched Julio bristle at Coach Turner's comment.

"And," the coach continued, "I just wanted you to tell him—ah—I'll help him catch up with the work he missed if he comes back."

"I'd tell him, if I knew where he was," Julio said. "It seems as if somebody called the cops on him, and he decided it just wasn't safe to stick around and find out what would happen. We haven't seen him, either."

"He threatened me," Turner said. "What was I supposed to do? Just ignore it?"

"Well, you had a number of choices," Julio said. "Talking to him was one of them. He's a real pussycat, you know. He's not like the rest of us," he added sarcastically.

"Okay, so I thought I'd just teach him a little lesson," Turner said. "I didn't mean to scare him into running away."

"Miguel couldn't afford to wait around and find out just how scared you wanted him to be," Julio said.

The coach looked at Julio for a long moment and blanched. "He's an illegal alien, isn't he?"

"Yeah, he's illegal," Julio admitted. "What's the difference if you know now? By this time, he's probably back in Mexico starving to death, anyway. So, if you inform on him, it really wouldn't matter all that much, anyway."

"If he comes back. If you find him," Turner said slowly, "I won't turn him in. I'm not sure what I can do, since this isn't exactly a cause I'm interested in, in general, but—I'll try to help Miguel, if I can."

Julio just stood there looking at the coach, obviously unable to grasp what he had just heard. Cass poked him and said, "Thanks. Thanks a lot."

"Yeah," Julio finally said. "Thanks."

They turned to walk away, but the coach called them back.

"Hey, Carothers and Martinez, don't you want to hear the good news?"

They turned back. "We were at the game, remember? We know the good news," Cass said, bewildered.

"Well, you know those two scouts who've been interested in you two? They were very impressed by what they saw tonight. They want to talk to both of you at the end of the season, as soon as it's legal.

Cass and Julio looked at each other, afraid to move one iota, afraid to speak.

"They want to ask you a few questions, such as, are you interested in playing on the women's team at UCLA, Carothers, and are you interested in playing for them, too, Martinez?"

"The women's team?" Martinez laughed. Then he and Cass jumped up and screamed. Cass was so happy and excited, she almost kissed the coach, but not even the good news would allow her to do anything that repulsive.

"Are you kidding?" Julio asked when they hit the ground.

"Hey, I wouldn't kid about that," the coach answered. "One more question," he said, looking around the empty parking lot. "Either of you fellas need a ride home?"

Cass started to laugh and squeezed Julio's hand. "I guess 'fella' is better than 'broad.'"

CHAPTER TWENTY-TWO

"Okay," Coach Turner said when they got to the bottom of the canyon. "All out. This is as far as this old clunker goes."

"Thanks, Coach," Cass said, getting out of the car. "We can make it up the hill from here."

Julio bounded out of the car after her, and they started up the canyon toward Cass's house. Julio looked up at the sky . "It looks like it's gonna start again," he said, zipping up his jacket. "I'm going to have trouble hitching back to town."

"I guess you'll just have to spend the night," Cass said, without looking at him.

"You mean at your house?" Julio asked, shocked.

"Unless you know someone else who lives up here," Cass answered, still not looking at him.

"No. No, I don't know anyone else up here," Julio said quickly. "But what are your parents gonna say? I mean—me—spending the night? Won't they go crazy?"

"No," Cass said, smiling.

Julio took her hand and held it in his. To her surprise, his hand was soft and warm.

"I can't believe that," Julio said laughing.

"And my parents can't believe I've never fought in the sexual revolution," Cass said, laughing with him. "They'll be relieved to see me with a guy someplace besides the basketball court."

"Even a Mexican guy?" Julio asked tentatively.

"Even better," Cass said, giving his hand a squeeze. "Since neither of them has gotten over being plain old Protestant American. Sky said she had hoped the Saint was at least half-Jewish when she met him, and Saint said he thought my mother was part Latino. Which part I don't know, of course, since she has blond hair and blue eyes like me. Anyway, they were both so disappointed to learn that neither of them was anything exotic, they almost stopped dating."

"Come on," Julio laughed. "You're putting me on."

"I wish I were," Cass laughed. "Wait till you meet them. You'll see."

By the time Cass and Julio reached the house, Julio had his arm around her, and they began to feel very close and comfortable together.

"You can sleep in my dad's workshop," Cass said. "It's nice and cozy. There's a bed, lots of blankets, heat, the works."

Julio followed Cass into the workshop and ran his hand over several pieces of furniture the Saint was working on, while Cass got out some extra blankets and a pillow. After the bed was made up, they looked at each other, both suddenly shy. Cass didn't want to leave the workshop and go into the house. She wasn't ready to climb into her cold bed just yet, especially since it was so nice and warm in here.

"I guess I'll go inside," she said, but she didn't move.

"The furniture is beautiful," Julio said. "Does your father make it, himself?"

"Oh, yes," Cass said eagerly, walking over to a table her father was working on and running her hand along the top of it. "At least, he makes some of it. Like this table. Some of it he just refinishes."

Julio walked over to the table and stood beside Cass.

He ran his hand along the top of it, also. They didn't really look at each other, but they were both very obviously aware of the other's presence. Almost accidentally, their hands met on top of the table, but neither of them pulled back. Julio slowly put his hand on top of Cass's, and at the same time they turned to look at each other, still shy and a little awkward.

"It's nice in here," Julio said, brushing back some stray hair from Cass's face.

"Yeah," she agreed. "Nice and warm."

She unbuttoned her jacket and threw it on the bed. Julio unbuttoned his jacket, too.

"Do you have to go to your house right away?" he asked.

"I can stay for a while, if you're not too tired. You played a hard game," she said softly.

"Stay," he said, taking her face in his hands and kissing her on the mouth.

Finally! she thought. Finally. But she didn't say anything, not a word, because she was afraid he might stop kissing her.

Julio didn't stop. He kissed her again and again, and they moved closer and closer together. Not even a single hair could fit between their bodies as they moved to the bed.

Cass had never in her life felt this way. She had dreamed about what it might feel like. She had thought about it, read about it, listened to records which sang about it, but it wasn't the same thing as experiencing it herself. She was so warm she could feel the heat of her face and body reflected in Julio's face and body— or maybe he was just as warm as she was, and they were creating this wonderful heat together.

Her eyes were closed tightly. She was afraid if she opened them, she would find out she was dreaming, and no one was in the room but her. She was afraid if she opened her eyes, Julio would disappear, so she kept them tightly shut and visualized his face as it melted into hers.

"Cass," Julio breathed softly as they sank against the pillows.

She wanted to get as close to him as possible and lose herself in him.

"ACHEW! ACHEW! ACHEW!" they heard, and they pulled apart as if someone had shot them both. They sat up on the bed, then froze in place. "ACHEW!" they heard again, then red-faced and sniffling, Miguel crawled out from under the bed.

"Miguel," they cried, leaping off the bed and hugging him, laughing and crying, and throwing a million questions at him at the same time.

After things got back to normal (well, actually, they would never be normal again, Cass thought, which was okay with her since she wasn't used to normal anyway), Miguel explained to them what he had been doing.

"So I see the police," he said. "And I'm scared to death. I don't know where to go or what to do. First, I run down to the pier where all the Mexican guys hang out and fish, thinking I'll find someone I know to help me, but then I think I must be crazy. It's already nighttime, and no one's fishing, now. But I'm at the ocean, and I'm thinking where I should hide, and I remember that Cass said she lived off the ocean highway, so I look up her address and I ask where is Topanga Canyon. Then I hitch a ride to the bottom of the hill. I get here, and no one's home," he continues.

"Sure, jerk," Julio said laughing. "We were out looking for you."

"And I'm pretty hungry since I haven't eaten anything since lunchtime, so I look around and I see this terrific garden, so I pick some stuff and eat it. Then I see a light on in here. I walk around and look in. I see it's some kind of workshop, so I come in and make myself comfortable and decide to wait for you to come back. I wait and wait. No one comes home. Finally, I fall asleep, but suddenly, I hear some noise outside, and like a rabbit, I jump under the bed. Just as I'm crawling under, these two people come in and fall down on the bed. Wham! One of them must have been a moose or something 'cause the whole bed sank, and I could barely move or breathe."

"A Fish," Cass laughed.

"What?" Miguel asked, confused.

"He was a Fish, not a moose. A Tuna Fish."

"Right," Miguel said sarcastically.

"Well, they thought you were a mouse," she laughed, teasing him.

"No wonder," Miguel laughed. "I was squirming around under there, afraid they were going to crush me. Finally, they got up and left. I don't know what they were doing in here, but they never came back, so I just stayed around here and lived off the food in the garden."

"But why didn't you come to the house?" Cass asked.

"Because I figured this was a good place to hide till no one was looking for me anymore, and I already got you into enough trouble, and I thought—"

"Oh, Miguel, you dope. We're so happy to see you," Cass said, hugging him again.

"Even if my timing's not so good," he said, blushing.

"Even if you're timing's not so good," Julio reassured him.

"I got caught in the rain, before, and there was all this commotion out there, so I couldn't get back in here, and I got soaked." He sneezed again, and they all laughed.

"Miguel, I just can't believe you're here," Cass said. "We were so worried about you. You really drove us crazy."

"Well, I don't want to continue to drive you crazy," Miguel said, "so I have a good idea. Since this was just a party for two before I interrupted you, I'll crawl back under the bed, and you can continue where you left off. Don't pay any attention to me. I'm real tired. I have this cold, and—"

"Miguel!" Cass and Julio said at the same time, pushing him onto the bed and sitting down on either side of him. They all leaned against the wall. Three friends just feeling good.

About the Author

Marilyn Levy is a prize-winning producer of children's TV who teaches senior English at a high school in Santa Monica, California.